The
Folk
Keeper

The Folk Keeper

Franny Billingsley

BLOOMSBURY

LONDON BERLIN NEW YORK SYDNEY

Bloomsbury Publishing, London, Berlin, New York and Sydney

First published in Great Britain in 2003 by Bloomsbury Publishing Plc
36 Soho Square, London, W1D 3QY

This paperback edition published in April 2011

First published in America in 1999 by Atheneum Books for Young Readers
An imprint of Simon & Schuster Children's Publishing Division, New York

A CIP catalogue record of this book is available from the British Library

ISBN 978 1 4088 1319 5

FSC
www.fsc.org
MIX
Paper from
responsible sources
FSC® C018072

Printed in Great Britain by Clays Ltd, St Ives plc

10 9 8 7 6 5 4 3 2 1

To my daughter Miranda, who found me the book that got me into the caves, and to my editor Jean Karl, who showed me the way back out.

Contents

1

From *Candlemas* to the *Feast of Saint Lancet*

February 2—Candlemas

It is a day of yellow fog, and the Folk are hungry. They ate the lamb I brought them, picking the bones clean and leaving them outside the Folk Door.

The lamb was meant for Matron's Sunday supper. She'll know I took it, but she will not dare say anything. She can keep her tapestries and silks and Sunday dinners. Here in the Cellar, I control the Folk. Here, I'm queen of the world.

February 4—Feast of Saint Lancet

I won't go, not upstairs, not yet.

A Great Lady has sent for me, says Matron, but what do I care for that? No one will fetch me from the Cellar. They're all too afraid of the Folk.

So I delight in slowly turning the crisp pages of my new Folk Record. I delight in very slowly recording the activities of the Folk. I will keep the Great Lady waiting as long as I please. The Folk have consumed:

> One bucket of milk, with plenty of cream
> One barrel of salt pork.

They've worked no mischief for months. The hens go on peacefully laying, the tomatoes happily growing. I wager I'm the only Folk Keeper in the city of Rhysbridge—in all of the Mainland, for that matter—who sits with the Folk for hour upon hour in the dark, drawing off their anger as a lightning rod draws off lightning. I am like the lightning, too; I am never injured. I know how to protect myself.

With every word, I keep the Great Lady waiting. Now she'll never want to take me from my Cellar. This is where I belong, me, Corinna Stonewall, on the chilly floor, keeping my Record by flickering candlelight. This is my only home—these stone walls, the Folk Door, the Folk in the Caverns beyond.

The Great Lady is now pacing the floor perhaps, asking Matron, *Where is Corin, Corin Stonewall?*

Corin, indeed! They don't know my secrets.

February 5

It's not a feast day, and the Folk have made no mischief, but yet I write. My astonishment spills into this Record as I wait for the Great Lady to call me. It will soon be time to go.

I shall miss this Cellar, my very own Cellar. I press my hand to the stone, loving the way moisture oozes to the surface. The Folk devoured the eggs and dried fish I left for them last night, and my last act for the Folk of the Rhysbridge Foundling Home will be to steal Matron's breakfast sausage.

It feels odd to write of myself, not of the Folk. Odd to take the pages of this Record above ground, to yesterday, when I slipped out the Cellar door and Matron grasped my collar. "You've kept us waiting!" She would have shaken me, but she was too afraid. I make sure of that.

The landing was dark; Matron's black silks seem always to absorb the light. She pointed to my Folk Bag, but did not quite touch it. "You don't need that!"

I stared at her. A Folk Keeper may carry his Bag wherever he pleases. She dropped her eyes at last. "Come along!"

There is power in silence, I have always known that.

I stumbled up the curling stone steps, into the smell of Matron's cheap tallow candles. Does she never notice her drawing room smells faintly of sheep?

"Make your bow to the Lady Alicia." Matron tapped the small of my back.

At first all I saw was smoky yellow light and blue velvet and topaz; then the Lady herself came clear. I don't care for beauty, not in the ordinary way, but she was something quite out of the ordinary. Rich chestnut hair, snapping black eyes, a creamy neck rising from a circlet of golden jewels. I was tempted to reach out to see if they would burn, but that would have been childish. I am never childish.

"Your bow!" cried Matron.

"We won't insist on the bow." Lady Alicia gazed at me as though I might be just as interesting to her. "They say you're fifteen, but you can't be more than eleven, can you, child?"

"I am small for my age," I said. "And weak. Moreover, I am clumsy and have a bad disposition."

"Quiet!" said Matron in a dreadful voice. "I can't help it, My Lady, if he doesn't eat. I'll have you know our foundlings take three good meals."

Matron neglected to mention that not all the meals are taken on the same day, but I didn't care about that. "I don't need to eat."

"An economical addition to our household," said a third voice, and a man stepped from the curtained recess of the window. He was perhaps as old as forty, with an ivory angel face and glossy black curls. The rest of him was black and white, too, all satin and lace. Rather a dandy, which I despise, but at least Matron must know how tawdry she looked beside him.

"Even supposing he's the right age," said the man, "there's another, bigger problem. We came expecting to find a girl."

"My husband instructed Sir Edward and me to fetch a Corinna Stonewall," said Lady Alicia. "*Corin* and *Corinna* sound alike but turn out to be quite different things."

What a dreadful sinking feeling came over me then. After four years of passing as Corin, I thought I'd never be caught. No one ever suspects a Folk Keeper could be a girl.

"We have only a Corin," said Matron. "You wouldn't want him, lazy good-for-nothing. He lets the Folk spoil the milk and rot the cabbage."

"I do not!" I snapped my lips shut. Matron didn't want me to leave; I was the best Folk Keeper she'd ever had.

But I didn't want to leave, either. I remembered too well the endless carrying of water buckets and scrubbing of floors and humiliations of Corinna before I burned my skirts and turned into a boy, and a Folk Keeper.

Lady Alicia put out her hand. "Won't you come see my husband? Only he can say if you're the child he's seeking. We've come all the way from Cliffsend, and he's very ill."

"What is that to me?" But I couldn't help thinking of the stories of Cliffsend, the largest of the Northern Isles, running with miles of underground caverns. The Folk there are said to be fierce and wild, drawing great strength from the stone all around. The Isles have more than their share of the Otherfolk—Boglemen and Sealfolk and Hill Hounds—as well as the Folk themselves, which are to be found everywhere.

"You'll get nothing but trouble from the lad," said Matron.

"I'll see your husband," I said to Lady Alicia, although I'd make sure I wasn't the child he wanted. Matron would learn she couldn't lie about me. But I never spoke my anger; no, you must never give your anger away.

Lady Alicia's carriage was crimson with a gold coat of arms on the door. Everything belonged to her, I gathered. Sir Edward, for all his fine clothes, was but His Lordship's cousin, related to the Lady by marriage. I slid about on the hard seats as the carriage rattled first through the familiar press of houses, each rubbing shoulders with its neighbors, into an unfamiliar world of grander homes and fewer shops. We drew up before an inn, entered through a red and silver parlor. A soft carpet wound up the stairs, and we wound up along with it.

"Hartley!" called Lady Alicia softly as we entered a dim room. She drew aside the velvet hangings of a massive bed. "We found a Corin for you, Hartley. There was no Corinna."

Lady Alicia was married to that old man! So old, and so disagreeable to look at, too, with a sharp watchful face and lips the color of bruises. The Lady drew me into the bitter smell of herbal plasters and bade me stand very close. Lord Merton's pale eyes hung on my face. It took him only a moment.

"Got you! And not a minute too soon."

"But he's not a girl!" said Lady Alicia.

"I'd recognize that face anywhere," said His Lordship. "I was misinformed about his sex, but girl or boy, this is the face I want. Leave us alone together."

Got you! I kept thinking as the door clicked shut. *Got you!* That had given me a nasty shock, but nothing like so nasty as when his arm shot out and his fingers circled my wrist. "Corinna!"

"It's Corin!" I said, pulling back. "Corin Stonewall."

But his grip was like death. Perhaps it was death, starting in his marble hands, working inward from blue-tipped fingers, leaving a pattering of bruises as it went.

"Now that I've got you," he said, "I will keep you! You shall come with us to Cliffsend."

"I won't! I'll never leave my Folk." I refuse to become a curiosity in some grand Manor. I know the gentry collect Folk Keepers and show them off, like jeweled snuffboxes. But a mere showpiece has no power, and without power—well, even in rocky Cliffsend, there's still scrubbing to be done; and daily doses of humiliation are to be found everywhere.

"I always get my own way," he said.

"So do I!"

I don't know if I glared at him, but he certainly glared at me. Twenty long seconds passed, and as though he could read my mind, he said, "I know you well enough to know you're counting out the time. Tell me the hour. Corinna, what's the time?"

"I'm Corin, I tell you!" I jerked back, but those hideous fingers held tight. "You said yourself you were misinformed. Are you blind? There's no Corinna here!"

"Blind, no," he said, "but the darkness is coming for me fast. I did you the favor of playing your game with you. Now you do me the favor of telling me the time. You always know the time, Corinna."

How can he know that? That is one of my secrets.

"Corinna, the time!"

I looked into myself, into that inexplicable built-in clock that ticks off the seconds running through my blood. "Sixteen minutes past four o'clock."

"You shall come with us to Cliffsend."

"I will bring you such trouble," I said. "You wouldn't want me there."

"Oh, but I would," he said. "All the trouble will belong to my good Lady and my cousin, for by then I'll be dead and gone. Corinna, what's the time!"

"Seventeen minutes past the hour."

He turned my hand, then stared at my wrist. "Yes, the same skin. There can be no doubt."

"The same skin as whose?" My skin is the most striking

7

thing about me—since I cut my hair, that is, which now merely puffs out from my head like a silvery dandelion. My skin is very white, and if you were fanciful (which I am not), you might say it was translucent, a window of milk glass skimming a blue filigree of veins.

"I knew your parents. You resemble your mother remarkably. I remember how in a dim room those green eyes of hers turned silver, like mirrors." The old man hesitated as though he might say something more, then swallowed his words back down, where I hope they poisoned him.

"What do you want of me?" I said.

"Your father was very ill," said the old man. "Just before he died, he told me of your existence, of his shame that he placed you in a foundling home. He entreated me to rescue you, bring you up as a lady. How did you become a boy, Corinna, and a Folk Keeper?"

"I changed my name on the Foundling Certificate. It's been four years now."

But I said no more. He needn't know I was sent to the Rhysbridge Home with a shipment of other orphans, including one boy who had apprenticed to become the Home's new Folk Keeper. He needn't know I took advantage of being unknown to them all to steal a pair of breeches, cut my hair, and turn myself into Corin. I will never tell anyone how I frightened the new Folk Keeper so dreadfully his very first night in the Cellar that he fled. I do not like to think of what I did—of how he screamed!—but I force myself to write it. I cannot let myself go soft.

"Do you tend the Folk well?" said His Lordship.

I nodded. The Rhysbridge Home could not have done

better, with me as the new Folk Keeper. I was denied the chance to apprentice, as a boy would have, but still, I've done better than most. I have pluck, nerve, patience, and an instinct for charms of protection.

"I have the power of The Last Word," I said.

There was a little silence. Not one in fifty Folk Keepers has that enormous power. "You have the power of The Last Word!"

I looked him in the eye, as you must do when you are lying. "I have that power."

But I must tell the truth here, although I was happy to tell Lord Merton all the lies I could summon. If I lied in this Folk Record, I wouldn't be able to trust it to give me an exact account of the activities of the Folk. I wouldn't be able to examine their behavior and puzzle out their patterns—when they might rage out of control, how best to turn aside their anger.

The truth is this: I do not have the power of The Last Word. Ever since I turned into Corin, I can no longer put together words that scan and rhyme. Only those rhyming words, springing of themselves into the Folk Keeper's mind, can extinguish the destructive power of the Folk. In The Last Word they sense a power greater than their own. But every rhyme that comes to me now has a hole in its middle, right where the heartbeat should be.

"You look like a boy," said Lord Merton.

"I know I do." Even at fifteen, I do not make a bad boy, all skin and bones and angles and awkwardnesses.

"You can choose to be raised as a gentleman," said His Lordship. "You needn't be a lady if you don't like."

"I won't be a gentleman, either." Even a gentleman

may be without power. As a Folk Keeper, I reign over the Cellar. I am indispensable.

"But your father was a gentleman!"

"What gentleman would leave a baby outside the Foundling Home with only a blanket and her name and birthday written on a scrap of paper? Who was he, this gentleman?"

But I already knew what Lord Merton's answer would be, that he was sworn not to reveal my parents' identity. That's always the way of it. No one wants to acknowledge a bastard child. But I was glad not to know. That way I could still imagine my mother was a magical creature, not some commonplace laundress with red hands. I could still explain my secret powers. Why I am never cold. Why my heart beats in harmony to some invisible clock. Why my hair grows two inches while I sleep. This last is inconvenient and hard to keep secret. But I learned not to tell. No one likes a child who may not be entirely human.

"Time is running out, Corinna. Come tell me, what's the time?"

"Thirty-three minutes past four o'clock."

"Come to Cliffsend as our Folk Keeper as well as one of us." His voice was so soft I had to bend close to hear. But his grip on my wrist was still tight. I could not help but admire him, for he is strong in his soul, as I am.

"How many households would depend on me?"

"Conscientious to a fault!" Lord Merton made a sound that might have been a laugh if he'd been stronger. "Not households, but a vast estate. It's not a simple matter of keeping the Folk from frightening the hens or spoiling the milk. Our Folk Keeper must make sure the

Folk interfere with none of the business of the estate, from lambing to ploughing to sowing to harvesting. You would answer to both Lady Alicia, who will be mistress there, and to my cousin Edward, who will act as her steward."

This was power beyond any I could have in Rhysbridge. A great estate that could not do without me! Impossible, then, ever to return to life as a drudge.

"So you will come?"

"I will think about it." But I am going, of course.

"Time is running out. Say you will come! Tell Lady Alicia I promised you the position of Folk Keeper as well as a place at the table. Tell her I promised in the name of the Lady Rona. Remember that, *the Lady Rona*. Corinna, what's the time?"

"Thirty-eight minutes past."

He was running down quickly now, I could see it. Surely as an unwound clock, he was running out of life. I would have to fetch someone to cover the mirror against Soulsucker, which would be here soon.

"It's very dark, now. What's the time?" Lord Merton's blue-tipped fingers fell from my wrist at last and lay curled in his palm.

"Thirty-nine minutes past."

"The darkness is the worst I've ever seen."

I watched him ebb away then, breathing still, but his mind overcome by darkness. *Got you!* I thought. Death had gotten him before he knew that he had gotten me, and it was still thirty-nine minutes past.

2

From the *Day of the Seven Spirits* Through *Bledstone Day*

February 6—Day of the Seven Spirits

No one can tell a falsehood about Corinna Stonewall and remain unpunished. Matron should have known that. She should have known I'd take a fierce revenge. You have to. The world will otherwise use you shamefully.

I spent my last moments in Rhysbridge watching to see what might result of my revenge. I glanced back at the Home as I followed the velvet cloaks of Lady Alicia and Sir Edward through the yellow fog. Sir Edward's Valet kept urging me on. He was scornful and splendid in striped crimson livery and powdered curls, but not even he could avoid the soot falling from the chimney pots, the mud, ankle deep. The crimson coach gleamed above the muddy world, and there was a black coach to go with it, with matching black horses. Lord Merton's body would follow us to Cliffsend.

I slipped on the high carriage step; the Valet grasped the scruff of my jacket and tossed me in. His fingers were puffy, like dough.

"Clumsy!" He clicked his tongue.

It is true that I can trip over anything and nothing—a speck of dust, a patch of sunlight, an idea. I move through life like a person with one eye, through a landscape that looks flat, but is really tricked out with hidden depths and shallows. It didn't used to be so, but no matter. I navigate the world well enough in my own way.

As we sat in the carriage, waiting to depart, Sir Edward and Lady Alicia wanted only to be talking of Lord Merton's decision, to take me in not only as a family member, but also to appoint me as Folk Keeper. They were uneasy, and why not? Matron told them I don't properly tend the Folk.

I let them assume I'd had a proper apprenticeship in the Foundling Home. They'll never know I'd bribed one of the lads to teach me reading and writing. I did his chores for a year. Another lad I bribed to teach me all he knew about spells of protection. I was two years doing his chores. The rest I picked up by keeping my ears open and hanging about the wise women and the fortune-tellers at the Rhysbridge market.

Still, Lady Alicia and Sir Edward asked me questions about keeping the Folk that any child could answer. I replied as I gazed back toward the Home, waiting to see my revenge begin.

Yes, I know to feed the Folk once a day.

Yes, I know they eat only of and from animals: meat, eggs, milk. After all, those are the only things of the human world they have the magical power to harm without stirring from their dark Caverns. They can harm those, and any planted crops, rooted in the soil under which they live.

Yes, I know a Folk Keeper must pass as much time as possible in the Cellar, so when the Folk grow wild, they spend their anger on him rather than on the crops and livestock.

Yes, I know they grow more wild and dangerous on holy days, which is when it is most important to keep the Record. The Folk are ever fighting the power of our Saints.

It was Sir Edward, still all in black and white, who said, "But will you be prepared for their unpredictability, that they can make mischief even on ordinary days?"

I pointed to the circlet of nails I wear about my neck. Cold iron, an antidote to stone, an antidote to the strength the Folk draw from the rock all around them.

"I do not go unprotected." I looked at my Folk Bag. Let them think it was brimful of charms instead of the rather ordinary items a Folk Keeper carries always: this Folk Record, and a bit of lead to write with; candles and a tinderbox, all wrapped in oilcloth against the Cellar's damp. A separate muslin sack held a dozen bits of old bread and biscuit, and I go nowhere without my shears. Perhaps no other Folk Keeper has hair that grows two inches a night.

"But he should know of the very particular danger," said Lady Alicia. Her maid was counting an extraordinary number of parcels and bandboxes, and I was glad of it, for it delayed our departure; I could still watch the Home.

"I already know the Folk of the rocky lands are especially strong and fierce," I said.

"Do you know," said Sir Edward, "that our last Folk Keeper, Old Francis, all but died of the Folk? It was before we left on this extraordinary journey." He said *extraordinary* as though it were a curse. "I have been sick with worry about leaving the estate with no skilled Folk Keeper in charge."

I shrugged. What of it? I was not afraid.

"Listen to Sir Edward," said Lady Alicia. "He knows the ways of the estate better than anyone."

"What shape are the Folk?" said Sir Edward.

I turned away from the window. "Everybody knows that not even a Folk Keeper can see them, as the Folk cannot bear the light!"

"Ah, but you can feel them. Old Francis felt them. It was weeks before we knew he'd live through the paralysis. *They are mostly mouth,* he said. *Wet mouth and teeth.*"

"You only feel them," I said, "if you're weak enough to let them hurt you. Besides, I have words—words that rhyme and scan. They spring into my mind of themselves."

Their astonishment was all I could have wanted. "The power of The Last Word!" said Lady Alicia, and Sir Edward said, "This is why Hartley thought the boy would do as Folk Keeper."

"All original rhymes," I added, to make sure they understood. "Never the same one twice."

Lady Alicia's maid had finished fussing, and the carriage began to rattle forward. I pressed my face to the window. Yes, there, my revenge was unfolding itself, starting

15

at sixteen minutes past noon, with the butcher banging at Matron's door.

I had told the merchants of our borough that I was leaving as Folk Keeper. That, at least, was true. But I also told them Matron had no mind to retain a new Folk Keeper, which was not true. The hens would fail to lay, I said, the butter fail to churn.

An eye for an eye, or so the saying goes.

A lie for a lie, or so my saying goes.

Vengeance. It is not always as delicious as you anticipate, but you must not flinch from it. Otherwise the Matrons of the world would rule us all.

Good-bye Cellar; good-bye Folk. Will the new Folk Keeper come sit with you and keep you content, as I did? Or will he leave your food just outside the Folk Door and slip away? How Matron will curse when the milk spoils.

Everyone else is afraid. Only I am powerful.

February 8—Bledstone Day

The scornful Valet will be sorry, too.

I write this in the courtyard of a country tavern. There are fresh, wet smells all around, distracting me from thinking through ways to avenge myself on him. I don't think I ever truly breathed in Rhysbridge. The early light spreads over the wet cobblestones, blurring their edges and buttering them with gold.

Two days have put Rhysbridge far behind. We rattled north on the King's Highway; all the other carriages pulled aside to let the black hearse by. Not everyone would be happy, as I am, to travel north, where the Folk are especially fierce. But although there's less stone in the south, and the Folk are correspondingly milder, the southlands have their share of dangerous Otherfolk. I, for one, would not like to stumble over an elvish ring, or meet the Headless Trunk.

The rolling hills and tidy farms have already given way to lonely tracts of juniper and rocky outcroppings. We go at a terrific rate even on these country roads, and the shepherds draw their flocks aside to let us pass. By evening, all this will give way to the sea.

The flow of air along my cheek has taken on a predictable sea pattern. The breezes flow inland during the day, then return to the sea at night. No one else seems to notice, and I do not mention it. Perhaps it is another secret power.

The others are all still in the gloomy tavern, with its heavy beams and smoke-stained walls, while I am out, breathing in the wet. They are still eating no doubt—eating, eating, always eating—today a great breakfast of smoked meat and pickled eggs and bread and butter. A cup of ale for Sir Edward. He bears no signs of travel, not that one, always immaculate in black and white. It is his Valet who keeps him so.

Yes, the Valet. I will have to work out my vengeance for what happened this morning, at breakfast, when I ate only a bit of meat, then wrapped the rest in a scrap of oiled paper. It would travel well and please the Folk of Marblehaugh Park.

"Whatever are you doing?" said Sir Edward.

"Gathering provisions for the Folk."

Such protests then! Sir Edward and Lady Alicia crying out that I must eat the meat myself! That Cook at Marblehaugh Park would give me all I need for the Folk! That I weigh no more than the scrap a dog might leave behind!

I still don't know whether to believe them. "You don't mean to say you *give* me food for the Folk!"

Lady Alicia seemed equally amazed. "You've been saving your food for the Folk, all these years?"

"That is the way of the Rhysbridge Home."

"We'll give you the same again for the Folk, and more," said Sir Edward. "We, too, want the Folk content and mild."

I dropped a bit of bread into my Folk Bag. There was an edge to Sir Edward's voice now. "Do you mean to disobey? Eat the bread or leave it be!"

I reached for another piece. The bread was protection from the Folk, who cannot abide the stuff. But before I could stow it in my Folk Bag, safe from the reach of human hands, doughy fingers snatched it from me.

"Clumsy!" said the Valet.

I buckled my Bag closed and left the tavern. No one—no one!—can say how I provision my Folk Bag.

The coachman's bugle is about to blow. The crimson coach will set off again, followed by the black hearse carrying His Lordship—His Lordship and the gold coins, one on each dead eye. And this is what I swear: The Valet will feel my vengeance before we reach Cliffsend.

February 8—ten minutes later

I have lost one of my secret powers. I discovered it just now when I climbed into the carriage.

"We've a quarter hour yet, Master Corin," said the coachman.

"A quarter hour? That can't be."

But it can. The coachman showed me his watch, and to be sure, I consulted the clock in the tavern.

I used to be so sure of the hour. My heart pumped out the seconds, which went ticking through my body, meeting other seconds, clustering into minutes, crowding into hours, into days. But now . . . Will my skin grow chilled, just like ordinary people? Will my hair refuse to grow at its prodigious rate?

My secret powers make up for that missing piece of me. I don't know what it is, but I ache for it each day. It's as though I have eyes, but there are colors I cannot see. As though I have ears, but there's a range of notes I cannot hear. But at least my powers set me apart from the rest. Once they are gone, will there be anything left?

February 8—evening

How can I describe the sea? It is stronger than anything, announcing its presence miles away, steeping the carriage with salt-and-seaweed fumes that sparked invisible stirrings behind my cheekbones. And the slow, steady singing of it . . . Now, in my room at the inn, my hair rises and the sea-song shivers over my scalp.

It reminds me of my old childish fancies, when I was still Corinna of the long silver hair. I used to think my hair was magic. I used to think it crackled with the shape of life, that with it I could catch the currents of the earth.

But when I turned into Corin, I gave up all my foolish ideas. They will not help you survive.

Sir Edward was in a pickle of impatience. He leapt from the carriage before it had quite stopped, which seemed a waste of heroics, as we are not to sail for Cliffsend until tomorrow. Not even Sir Edward can hurry along the night.

I waited until the wheels no longer rattled over the stones. I am not made for leaping from anything that moves.

There was the sea at last, stretching into infinity. Seagulls floated on the water, feathered whitecaps dotting the waves. Everywhere there was spit and spray, and where the waves had nothing to dash against, they crashed into themselves and curled back into the sea.

Behind me rose the usual arriving-at-an-inn noises. There were instructions about supper, instructions about attending to the horses, instructions to the Valet from Sir Edward. "I shall want a clean neck cloth, and a fresh shirt as well."

I knew then what my vengeance would be. The luggage had been set upon the ground, and it was easy, while the others were all so busy, to loose the fastenings of Sir Edward's valise.

It did not take long. I stood with my back to the carriage, facing the sea, not watching, but listening.

There was a gasp from the Valet. I imagined those silks and satins, all in black and white, tumbling to the cobbles. Lady Alicia's maid gave a tiny squeak.

"Clumsy!" said Sir Edward.

Then I walked to the beach.

It was a fine, wild February night, with a keen wind shrieking past my ears. The beach has a language of its own, with its undulating ribbons of silt, the imponderable hieroglyphs of bird tracks. The receding waves catch on innumerable holes in the sand. Bubbles form and fade. A new language, with a new alphabet, which I will learn to read.

The sea up close is enormous. I squeezed my eyes against it for a moment, which is ridiculous, like fighting a giant with a pin. It comes to you anyway, through your ears and nose and skin and tongue. It is a savage, muscular thing, a vast dim wetness battering at the land and the air and all your senses.

A little dock leaned over the water. I leaned over with it, careful not to fall, as I swim only a little, dangling my hand into the waves. Quicksilver shapes flashed beneath. Idly, idly, my fingers drifted. I was at least as surprised as the fish when my fingers snapped round its thrashing body.

I pulled it from the water, feeling it turn inside my grasp. I smelled it, which was innocent enough, wasn't it, merely smelling a fish? But one thing leads to another, for I drew it near my nose, which is near my mouth, which then opened. I felt the fish struggling between my lips, my tongue curling eagerly to fold it in.

What was I doing! I flung it back.

Why did I almost devour it? I, who rarely need to eat, hungry for this thing of living flesh and blood? I refuse to be like ordinary people, living their ordinary, powerless lives, who need to eat and eat and eat.

I must be truthful to this Record. Even now, long after I tossed away the fish, I am still hungry for it. Perhaps I'm emptying out, my secret powers slowly ebbing. But when I look at myself now, by the clear light of real wax candles, all is just as usual, my skin almost transparent from the light shining through.

3

Cupid's Crossing

February 12—Cupid's Crossing

I scarcely recognize myself.

Whoever saw Corinna lying under a gilded ceiling, between blue velvet hangings? Lying in sheets that have been starched, and even pressed? The smell of leftover heat from the mangle lingers in them still.

As even my memory can fail—yes, even mine!—I've made it a rule to record events as they occur, not letting days go by. But I couldn't help breaking it; I am only now coming back to myself.

It seems much longer than three days ago when I waited in the early-morning dark to board the Cliffsend ferry. The cold moon was embedded in a hard sky, picking out the red caps and white canvas jackets of the fishermen, the pale fur trimming of Lady Alicia's streaming cloak. I didn't know ladies could run.

"Finian!" She flung her arms around a man you might at first take for a small bear, tall and broad and light on his feet.

"I wondered when you'd see me," he said.

I tried to puzzle out who he might be. His educated voice and elegant greatcoat went together, but not with his canvas fisherman's shoes.

"What are you doing here!" Lady Alicia kissed his cheek, then boxed his ears lightly.

Who can explain it? Humans are so odd.

"I missed you, of course." The young man paused.

"And you wanted an excuse for a long sail. You must have been up all night!"

"I don't need sleep," said Finian. "I have to be up and doing!" There came a little silence. "I am sorry for His Lordship's death. As usual, I say the right thing too late."

"Let's not quarrel today," said Lady Alicia finally. If she grieved for Lord Merton's death, she kept it close to herself. I like that in her. "Take *The Lady Rona,* and may you have fair winds and good speed."

The Lady Rona! The password Lord Merton had given me to assure my place as Folk Keeper. Strange to think *The Lady Rona* was merely a boat. But when I peered over the high stone jetty, I understood why you might remember her in landlocked Rhysbridge. She was such a pretty, graceful thing, particularly beside that lump of a ferry, which would doubtless bump over the sea much as the carriage had bumped over the rutted roads.

Then I, Corinna Stonewall, who never asks for anything, astonished myself by tugging at this stranger's coat. "I want to sail *The Lady Rona,* too!"

Bears are said to be fast. Before I could regret my words, Finian had whirled around. He knelt and held out his hand, which, like the rest of him, was enormous.

"A fellow sailor!" He had a curving beak of a nose, striking winged eyebrows, and dark-red hair.

"Not a sailor," said Lady Alicia. "Corin's our new Folk Keeper."

"A Folk Keeper?" said Finian. "But I thought . . ." His voice trailed off and he pulled a pair of spectacles from his pocket and shoved them on his nose.

"He has the power of The Last Word," said Lady Alicia.

I'm sure I stared at Finian as hard as he stared at me. I'd never seen such a young man wearing spectacles.

"I beg your pardon, Sir Folk Keeper," said Finian at last. "My eyes are playing me some tricks."

"Furthermore," said Lady Alicia, "he's the child Hartley was looking for."

"Then I'll be sure not to let him drown, Mother," said Finian meekly.

Mother! I stared at Lady Alicia, trying for the first time to guess her age.

"Everyone wonders the same thing," said Finian. "Here's a little hint. Her eldest son, and only son—that's me!—is twenty-one." He stretched out his hand and I stared at it.

"Shake it," he said. "Shake it and say 'Pleased to meet you!' and let's be off."

He followed his own command at once, dropping

effortlessly off the jetty and into the pretty boat. I stood looking down uncertainly, until Finian gave me his hand, which I all but stood on as he helped me down.

"May the Sealfolk swim unharmed!" cried Lady Alicia.

We shot away from the jetty. "The Sealfolk?" I said.

"Three drops of Sealfolk blood on the waters is enough to raise a storm. So you don't want to be sailing when one of them is harmed." I'd never heard that, for all my hanging about the Rhysbridge market. But then, there are no Sealfolk on the Mainland.

The sea is powerful enough without a storm. I felt its deep-running currents, the whole vast world of it, shuddering with life. Dawn had brought a silver sheen to the surface, mercury floating on fathoms of night. It's extraordinary when you think of it, sailing on those infinite waves with just a thin layer of wood between you and the world beneath.

Finian pressed something cool and round into my palm. I held it to the sky, which had been slowly brightening and was about to snuff out the moon. It was a bead, the color of honey. "Amber," he said.

"A gift to the sea," I said. "For smooth sailing."

"How do you know that?"

"A good Folk Keeper knows all about charms," I said, which is true, although most are schooled in them, while I ferret them out. I tossed the bead into the waves.

Finian looked at me a long time. "I suppose you do, at that. I can certainly believe you're casting a spell on me with those big green eyes." He laughed softly. "I hope it's a pleasant one. Listen, let's be friends. I have enough enemies already, although there's one gone now that His

Lordship's dead. Here then, Corin, what are you staring at?"

I have little family feeling myself, but I couldn't help thinking it was strange to speak of his father as an enemy, and before he was even buried!

"Not my father, my stepfather! I'm no Merton, but a Hawthorne. My real father died long ago, leaving me a title, but no land to go with it. My mother remarried only last year, and strange as it may seem, I believe she married for love. So here I am, Sir Finian Hawthorne, at your service, but I will box your ears if you call me *Sir*."

He was teasing. I know people—ordinary people—tease each other, but it felt queer to be teased myself. Should I permit it? After all, I am in no way ordinary.

"He was your enemy?"

"I like to speak broadly," said Finian. "It goes with the rest of me. He wasn't terribly happy I was to be the lord of Marblehaugh Park after my mother—although she'll doubtless outlive me by several hundred years."

"*You're* to be the lord of Marblehaugh Park?"

"It isn't polite to sound so surprised. Yes, my mother is mistress now, and I shall inherit after her. Too bad for me Lord Merton had no children by his first wife, for they would have inherited instead."

"Most people like to inherit," I said.

"But His Lordship didn't like me to indulge my passion for boats, sailing them and building them. I'd planned to have a shipyard someday, but he said that was no fitting ambition for a future lord. My mother stood behind his decision. It's hard to forgive her, even if I realize she's trying to learn the ways of the estate. Poor Finian!" He shook

26

his head in mock self-pity. "Poor Edward, too. Had he been a closer cousin to my stepfather, he would have had the estate."

But I was still thinking of what Finian had said before. "You can't build a ship if you like?"

"Pity, isn't it," he said. "Even Edward chides me sometimes for my inelegant interests. I wish I liked guns and loud bangs. That's an amusement worthy of a lord, it seems."

"I'd be ashamed to be you!" The heat in my voice surprised me. "Ashamed to let anyone stop me from having a shipyard if I liked, a great lad of twenty-one and a lord in the making."

I'd been a powerless foundling, yet hadn't I managed to escape the endless drudgery of my life? Hadn't I turned myself inside out, turned Corinna into Corin, to become a Folk Keeper?

"I am only a Folk Keeper, but I do as I like."

"Tell me how to do that!" said Finian.

I shrugged. I'd already said too much.

"Quite right," said Finian. "Why tell me for nothing? I propose an exchange." He was teasing and not teasing, all at once. "Tell me how to get what I want. Tell me that I *can* get what I want. I've almost lost all hope. Fill me with words of . . ." He paused.

"Conviction?"

"Conviction," said Finian. "I like that. You give me a Conviction every few days, to keep my spirits up."

"What do I get in return?"

"Name your price," said Finian.

"Secrets," I said.

"I beg your pardon?"

"Secrets, about Marblehaugh Park."

"A fair exchange." Finian looked as though he might laugh. Was this all a great joke to him? "My Secrets for your Convictions."

But it was not a joke to me. "Don't we exchange blood for a solemn pact?"

Finian closed his hands. "My fingertips are too precious. It will be just as binding without. Come, ask for your Secret."

"What does your mother love best of all?" It's when you know people's secret passions that you can get power over them if need be.

"I won't charge you a Conviction for that," said Finian. "It's no secret that she loves me!"

"What does Sir Edward love?"

"He loves Marblehaugh Park."

"That's hardly a secret, either," I said.

"Don't you want to know what I love best?" said Finian. I patted the boat. "I already know."

Finian laughed. "You shall see why. Take the tiller." He pressed a length of wood into my hand, telling me to hold it firmly, to *fall off* as the sails began to flap.

"I see!" I said, and I did. I pushed the tiller, and the sails belled out with the wind.

"Well!" said Finian.

Prisms of light skimmed the surface. A wave broke against us, and before it shook apart into splash and spray, I felt the strength of it, the hundreds of pounds smashing our boat. There were prisms in the spray, too, showering us with drops of light.

"You must have sailed before," said Finian.

"I first saw the sea yesterday night."

We were silent then a long time. He did not ask for the Conviction I owed him, nor did I offer it. The sun wheeled through the sky, pausing at the top when Finian took out a lunch of bread and cheese, plunging westward by the time we spied a mound of gray stone rising from the sea.

"The Seal Rock," said Finian. "We're almost to Cliffsend." Against the rock, waves shattered and turned to gauze.

"I see no seals."

"I'll call them for you," said Finian.

He drew a little whistle from his pocket. It was made of tin, but the music it made was at least silver, wrapping itself round me with an invisible lifeline.

Five sleek heads rose from the water. They are lovely things, the seals, so alert and intelligent they look as though they might speak. Huge eyes, ringed with black. Dark heads, silvered by the afternoon light.

"May our boat be blessed," said Finian.

My voice came as an echo. "May our boat be blessed." And even after the last note had died out over the water, every nerve along my spine stood on tiptoe to hear him play.

"Can you call the Sealfolk, too?" I have always loved the stories of the Sealfolk, who swim the sea as seals. Why, though, do they ever shed their Sealskins to walk the land as humans? If the skin should be lost or stolen, they can never return to the sea. I'd never risk losing any Cellar where I was Folk Keeper, the only place I truly belong.

"Surely you know how to call them," he said. "You with your knowledge of charms."

I did know that. "Seven tears shed into the sea at high tide to call the Sealfolk. But I have no tears."

"I'll lend you some of mine," said Finian. "I have plenty."

Suddenly the world paused, then turned itself inside out to run the other way.

"What has happened!" I cried. "What is happening?"

"What do you mean?" said Finian.

"Don't you feel it, everything turned round?"

Finian sniffed the air as though I were describing a smell. "The tide just turned, but you can't mean that?"

"No, I can't mean that." But I did. With Finian's words came a burst of understanding. I knew where my internal clock had gone wrong.

It is the tide that pulls the seconds through my blood. It is the tide that threads the minutes through my bones. But the Mainland tides are set to a different clock from those of the Northern Isles. I breathed in deeply, settling myself into the ebb of the sea.

I have more power than I know.

I will need it all, too. The Folk of Cliffsend must draw terrific strength from their stony home. The red cliffs of the western coast stretch easily for ten miles, and Finian said the whole island runs thirty miles across. There might be hundreds of miles of tunnels, all connecting underground. But much of the island is uninhabited (save for legions of Otherfolk). Just a handful of villages, and the Manor.

The cliffs reared hundreds of feet above the sea,

sculpted by the waves into spectacular shapes. "See there?" Finian pointed to a long, low scallop in the cliffs. "You'll see the Manor in a moment. The cliffs are just babies there, no more than fifteen feet high."

The Manor was enormous, even from a distance, a small castle almost, with turrets and spires and diamond-paned windows winking in the late sun. Behind everything rolled a treeless landscape of brown and purple heather.

We hugged the cliffs now, the waves rolling into smooth combers as we entered a sheltered bay. The cliffs yawned in around us, then curled out again to keep on with their job of holding back the sea. The beach was a semi-circular shelf of crumbled rock mixed with feathers and fish skeletons and broken shells. The retreating tide showed that the beach ended abruptly and turned into vertical cliff-face again. We docked at a pier of weathered silvery wood with a ladder up one side, for at low tide, Finian said, there was a long drop off the edge of the beach to the seafloor below.

There were thousands of birds, tens of thousands, nesting in the cliffs' shingled sides, wheeling through the air, screaming, plummeting into the water, and diving at my head. I don't blame them. I don't like strangers myself.

"Now you get to meet my sweetheart." Finian patted the overturned hull of a boat. "The *Windcuffer*. By spring, she'll be the prettiest, fastest little boat in Cliffsend."

"You're building her?"

Finian put a finger to his lips. "Repairing her. Don't tell my mother or Edward. We'll go sailing in her, you and I."

"I'll be spending my time in the Cellar," I said.

"So hellishly bored," muttered Finian. "Bored, and stuck. Up we go, Corin, so you can see our lovely home and sleep in our lovely beds and eat our lovely meals and tend our lovely Folk."

But the path up the cliff face was so narrow it might have been scratched in with a hat pin. "I can't, not with my Bag."

"I'll carry it for you."

"No other human can touch a Folk Keeper's Bag!"

"I won't look in the thing," said Finian. "Come along!"

But I hugged the Bag to me, not arguing (if you don't argue, you can't give in), just looking about and smelling the salt and dead fish—wonderfully good together, at least in small doses.

Finally Finian laughed a little. "Perhaps I won't be quite so bored with you about. I'll go on ahead and give you a hand."

I was dragged and bounced up the path behind Finian, setting off waterfalls of stone from the cliffs, but mere rivers of blood from my knees. A flock of gulls beat into the air with indignant cries.

"I'll leave you to catch your breath," said Finian, as I lay gasping on the cliff top. "It's my turn now to fetch my things from the beach. Don't move, else the Hill Hounds will get you! I'll be back in a moment to collect my Conviction. You needn't think I've forgotten."

But he was a great deal more than a moment, and at first I picked bits of stone from my hands, then blew on my knees, and finally I rose to look behind me.

The Manor was as spectacular as the cliffs. Huge

granite blocks of it stretched down the coast for quite as far as I wanted to walk. I wondered where the Cellar was; perhaps I could find a door. The park was astonishingly green and beautifully kept, as though the rugged landscape had been shaken out hard and laid down again as a carpet of grass.

There were plenty of windows, gray and flat in the waning light, but I saw no entrance to the Cellar. A long row of French doors caught my reflection just as a wild howling came from behind.

My feet exploded into a run before my mind could make sense of the howling. It was deep chested, savage, melancholy. The Hill Hounds, they were not just some jest of Finian's!

My feet pounded now into the grass, now into the loose stones of a circular carriage drive. I've always despised the foolish hero of the Otherfolk stories who breaks the rules to look over his shoulder. But I did, just the same; I couldn't not look behind, and the sight of a pack of muscular bodies was punishment enough. No ordinary dogs these, but Hill Hounds, cut from shades of dusk.

Face forward again, seeing a tree growing in the shelter of a wall. Even I could climb it, for like me, it was thin and stunted. One branch, two branches, then a yell, a tug at my breeches. I never felt the fall, but my head exploded with brilliant light.

"My Saints, it's Corin!" I knew that voice. "Fall off, lads! Fall off!"

I found myself staring into a white moon caught in a web of branches.

4

Saint Valentine's Eve to the Feast of Saint Valentine

February 13—Saint Valentine's Eve

I can sit up now without getting dizzy. The lump on my temple's no bigger than a goose egg, and my brain no longer feels as though it's been borrowed for a game of croquet. Tomorrow is a feast day, so I shall walk myself to the Cellar, the Cellar and the Folk. Mrs. Bains, who is my jailor (but says she is the housekeeper), has ordered me to stay in bed some days longer. But she doesn't know Corinna Stonewall!

How improved I am from the night of the hounds, when I awoke to the taste of blood, my own small sea of water and salt. The infinite weight of my eyelids pressed me into darkness, but small sounds rose all around. The crunch of stone, the sound of striking flint, a chorus of soft, quick sighs.

"I warned Corin about the Hill Hounds." It was Finian's voice, but very strange, like a bead rattling down a metal cone into the shell of my ear. "I should also have told him they're susceptible to the power of The Last Word."

The Last Word? Could it work against the Hill Hounds? I tried to speak, but the furniture of my mind had all been rearranged, my words neatly folded and stored out of sight.

"He's stirring!" said Sir Edward.

Yellow light swam through the tissue of my eyelids. I squinted them open.

Tall shadows stood behind the torchlight; panting shadows slid about their feet. "Silver eyes!" said Sir Edward. "He has silver eyes in the dark."

"Corin!" said Finian as my eyes began to slide closed. "Don't slip away again. Remember, you owe me a Conviction!"

"A what?" said Sir Edward.

"It's our secret," said Finian.

The moon still hung in the branches; loose stones pressed into my back. Everything was so very rocky here. The torchlight leaned closer; one of the shadows knelt and turned into white lace and black satin.

"At least they've not killed you!" said Sir Edward.

I found at last the place my words began. "I must tend to the Folk!"

"Don't trouble yourself about the Folk," said Finian.

"Never say that!" said Sir Edward.

The Finian shadow also knelt and turned itself into enormous fingers, which began very gently to feel my head.

"Where's my Folk Bag?"

"I have it here." Finian found the lump and hissed in sympathy. "Ouch! You'll have a headache for a week. Why did you go walking about? I told you about the Hill Hounds."

I smelled the salt spray in his hair. "The Last Word works against them?"

"You've been eavesdropping!" said Finian. "It's actually a family secret for which I should charge you a Conviction. But I'll give it to you free, as an apology for lingering so long on the beach. Yes, you can control our hounds with The Last Word, but mind you, they can be very fierce."

"So can I," I said, although it was hard to feel fierce on the long journey to the Manor. It comes back to me now as a jumble of pain sliced with a few vivid memories. A brisk, bossy voice saying Finian might carry me. A sickening surge as my head left the ground. Infinite tiny jolts over those infinite stones.

I bit at the inside of my mouth and squeezed my eyes shut, and all the while the owner of the bossy voice was urging Finian to be careful. "The boy weighs no more than a chicken, Mrs. Bains," he said, irritated at last. "I shan't drop him."

There were more voices then, and the heat and light of many candles. I opened my eyes to a press of faces. Servants in powdered wigs, Sir Edward's deep blue eyes, Finian's wild-winged eyebrows. At the corners of his eyes were little lines from squinting. Mrs. Bains, not brisk and angular like her voice, but with a great white biscuit of a face, stuck with two black currants.

Someone poured something nasty in my mouth. I tried

to spit it out, but a salt-spray hand wouldn't let me. The stuff burned down my throat and set a fire in my head.

A sludge of time oozed by until Mrs. Bains tried to undress me. Oh, then I came to life again, shouting, biting, kicking, striking something too solid to be Mrs. Bains.

"The boy's wild!" said Finian. "Let him be." And somehow, there I was, fully dressed, between the starched and mangled sheets shouting, "I need my shears!" Was my hair growing? They mustn't know it grows so fast.

"He's wandering," said Mrs. Bains. "I'll bring him a sleeping draught."

"I won't sleep!" I cried, for it is only then my hair grows.

Finian wrapped my arms around my Folk Bag. "Everything you brought is safe here."

"I still won't sleep!"

I didn't, either, although I could not quite stay awake. I was caught in a dim, cobwebbed place, my mind helpless against apprehension, fears breeding freely and multiplying.

I remember those days as a series of separate sketches. Finding myself lying on the dressing-room carpet for some reason, looking through the legs of the rosewood dressing stand. My memory is etched with an image of Cardomy Castle painted on the washing-up basin. And they had actually gilded the chamber pot!

Leaning against pillows, seeing my reflection in the mirror opposite. Broad, flat cheekbones, huge eyes set at a slant, a gray-yellow bruise on my temple, my hair grown a bit during unguarded fits of sleep.

Opening my eyes, thinking I'd been quite awake, but seeing that Finian had magically appeared. "Sleep, Corin. I'll save you from an attack of the Mrs. Bains!"

Rummaging in my Folk Bag during one lucid moment. It was undisturbed. I still had the candles, the tinderbox, this Record and my bit of writing lead, all properly wrapped in oilcloth. Also the bits and crusts of bread and the smoked meat from that Mainland tavern. Out came the shears, off came the hair, back I went to dandelion fuzz. I dragged myself to the fireplace and tossed in the cuttings. There was a bright flare and sizzle, the acrid smell of burning hair, and I was safe once more.

Almost safe. Once I am in the Cellar, proving myself indispensable to the safety of Marblehaugh Park, they'll never send me away. I will be safe then, absolutely safe.

February 14—Feast of Saint Valentine

At last I am where I belong. It is still early morning, but I have already been on a long journey. It was raining when I awoke, and very dark. The grand staircase forked from itself at the landing and met itself in the great hall below. The sconces were unlit. I made my way down by a thin, watery starlight.

It should be easy for a Folk Keeper to sink to the Cellar, water finding its own level. But the Manor was tricky, sending me down corridors, round corners, with nothing but more corridors and corners ahead. There came finally the sound of someone laying a fire.

My feet followed my ears, past a half-dozen doorways breathing cold sighs on my shoulders, to a doorway through which hundreds of eyes shone from bodiless heads. There was a deer with branching antlers; a fox with bright, sad eyes; a fish longer than I, smiling grimly.

Guns and loud bangs, Finian had said. *An amusement worthy of a lord.*

Then another, most peculiar trophy. My eye glanced over a tall-backed chair to a mirror above the mantle. In the glass was reflected Sir Edward's face. His lips opened. "Come in."

The fire crackled; a glow slid round the chair and along the walls, illuminating other trophies. Here were the bodies without heads. Some I recognized—that shaggy skin was surely a bear!—but what could that enormous blue-black one have been? What about that silvery skin, the size of a small goat, or a large dog?

"That will do," said Sir Edward, and the person lighting the fire shuffled round the chair and into sight.

Such a face I have never seen. One side of his mouth opened, stretched, smiled as mouths do, addressed me as Master Corin and said he was at my disposal. The other side was frozen, and the terrible paralysis didn't stop there but ran up his face and into his eye, trapping it neither open nor shut. It must have been difficult to lay the fire, for his left arm hung limp at his side.

I knew him at once: the Folk Keeper before me. Old Francis.

He had not grown old, he had been made old.

"Breakfast is not laid until seven o'clock," he added. The words fell from his stiff mouth like wooden blocks between us.

"I don't eat," I said, which is not quite what I meant,

but close enough to the truth. "I'm looking for the way to the Cellar."

"Old Francis will show you," said Sir Edward, rising at last, his mirror image turning into flesh and blood as he, too, appeared around the chair. He clapped sharply. "Come, lads. Liquorice, Honeycomb, make your apologies to Master Corin."

Two hounds slid past Sir Edward and sat at my feet, fawning in the contemptible way of dogs. Their heads rose past my waist; their eyes were yellow, their ears red.

"They won't attack once they know you," said Sir Edward. "Sniff him well, lads, take good note of our new Folk Keeper."

I lifted my hands from the hounds' warm breathing. I hid my fright, I think, hid how my heart leapt like a rabbit and staggered against the bony walls of my chest. "You didn't tell me you keep Hill Hounds."

"Finian likes to call them so," said Sir Edward. "But he also likes to exaggerate. Their ancestors bred with our hounds, and this generation is rather less than more of the Otherfolk."

But I wasn't sure. I remembered the savage melancholy of their voices. I remembered they are subject to the power of The Last Word.

"They're still wonderfully fierce," said Sir Edward. "See here." To my astonishment, he drew a pair of gloves from his pocket and flung them onto the carpet. "At it, lads!"

The hounds leapt upon them, savaging them silently. It seemed such a waste of good gloves, just as putting gold coins on Lord Merton's dead eyes had also seemed a waste, when coppers would have done just as well.

A third hound came to stand by me, as though to replace the others. He was very old, with a grizzled muzzle and watery eyes. "Fall off, Taffy," said Sir Edward. "You've no need to apologize." The dog lay down, very stiff in the hindquarters.

"It is a feast day," I said. "I cannot delay finding the Cellar." It was already eleven minutes past six.

"Old Francis knows the way well enough," said Sir Edward, which seemed rather cruel, but Old Francis merely bowed and said he'd be honored to escort me.

I could have found it on my own if I'd known to follow the smell of baking bread. The Cellar stairs were just outside the Kitchens. But Old Francis shuffled dutifully before me, then lit a candle from another candle, burning opposite the Cellar door. "This one's always kept burning. Our Folk Keepers sometimes need to reach the Cellar in a hurry."

The Cellar seemed like an old friend, although I was just now meeting it for the first time. The light from my taper illuminated the familiar rounded ceiling, the familiar wooden barrels—port, wine, brandy—the familiar whitewashed walls. The inner Cellar was smaller still, smelling damp and deep. Now I was home! I pressed my hand to the walls, felt the familiar homey chill, and also something peculiar etched into the stone.

I shone my light about. The walls were broken by words carved over and over again.

Over and over, they said the same thing:

> *Poor Rona: take pity on her.*
> *Poor Rona: take pity on her.*
> *Poor Rona: take pity on her.*

Again and again. *Poor Rona*. Perhaps the Lady Rona was more than a boat. Not even the most clever boat built by Finian could have written these words. How long had it taken this mysterious woman? Months? Years? What did she use? A nail?

I touched my own necklet of nails.

The carvings had been made long ago, for they'd been whitewashed over, and the whitewash was not recent. But you could see them easily when you knew to look.

Poor Rona. I felt sorry for her, whoever she was. But her passion to make her mark on these Cellar walls must have been a great inconvenience to the Folk Keeper.

The curving top of the Folk Door reached the middle of my forehead. Its crosswise bands of iron were clean and free of rust, likewise the hasps and handle. Not that it matters. The Folk will resist passing the sign of the cross, whether rusted or no.

I laid bits of old bread and biscuit in a circle before opening the Folk Door. Inside the circle, I would be safe. The Folk cannot cross a circle of bread, the Bread of Life. I left my candles and tinderbox in my Folk Bag, for Old Francis had given me a whole candle! I set the smoked meat in front of the Folk Door, then opened it a crack. And there came something I'd never felt in the Rhysbridge Home, a hum of dark energy shivering from behind the Door. It must be a strong energy to reach me in the Cellar, for the Folk would have to have drawn far back into the Caverns where my light could not shine.

I was not afraid. I am never afraid.

I have finished writing. I will soon snuff my candle and release the Folk from the Caverns. My thoughts float above ground, first to a room of shining eyes, then sail out to sea, to the boat ride with Finian. He said he would take me sailing again. I feel almost sorry I haven't the time.

The darkness is stirring behind the Door. The Folk are straining at the boundaries of my candlelight. I shall put it out now and meet the Folk of Marblehaugh Park.

5

Feast of Saint Valentine Through Mischief of All Sorts

February 14—Feast of Saint Valentine

The Folk consumed:

>All the smoked meat
>A smallish bit of Corinna Stonewall.

But I am one of the lucky ones. I am not paralyzed, I am not wasting away. No one need know, for my clothes hide the clusters of bruises, and I am armed with a new protection.

I have this newest charm from Cook. Pale, silent Cook—except when he curses—his eyes red-rimmed as though he's forever peeling onions. He tried to pour my charm into a cone of paper. "Damn sea air!" he muttered when it stuck and he had to go at it with a spoon. The cone is small to hold so vast a substance. Salt, Salt of

Eternity, workaday stuff to us, agony for one of the Folk.

I told Mrs. Bains I am not yet well enough to take supper with the others. I shall spend my evening in the Cellar instead.

February 15

My mouth turns bitter when I read yesterday's words. I thought I had all I needed, and more. Delicacies from Cook that would have made the Rhysbridge Folk swoon dead away. Why would these Folk not be content with smoked pheasant and turkey eggs and a tub of milk? I even stirred the milk a long while, blending in the cream. That's how they like it best.

But I opened the Folk Door to the same simmering energy, waiting only for darkness to allow it into the Cellar. I sat myself in double concentric rings of bread and salt. Damp seeped through my breeches. With my fingertips, I snuffed the candle.

Crash! The Door slammed against the wall. A tidal wave of power boiled across cold stone, then sucked itself back at the ring of salt.

The salt couldn't hold them off, I knew that even then, knew it couldn't contain that terrible force straining over the thin crystalline Ring of Eternity. I could perhaps have fled, many another Folk Keeper would. But in order to keep your place, you have to do your job well, drawing the anger of the Folk upon yourself, diverting it from the livestock and the crops.

There was a rush of power, crossing the salt with screams so shrill they bore into the webbed netting of my bones. Was this what Old Francis had felt, the cramping that doubled my toes to my heels, that pushed my shoulders to my lap? It mixed me all together with myself, my insides turning outward to meet my own translucent skin.

I did not cry out. I poured my screams into silent curses, blasting the Folk with my rage. Me, why me? I, who feed them and stir the milk and sit countless hours on the damp floor!

Foolish girl, Corinna. What are you thinking? The Folk have no hearts; they do not care for kindness.

February 16

I am finding the Lady Rona everywhere!

I found her again today at dusk when I visited the Marblehaugh Park churchyard. There was not much to visit, as it was no larger than a handkerchief, only a handful of gravestones and a little chapel, shoved against the seaward wall of the Manor.

I was looking for churchyard mold. I'd once heard it whispered that graveyard earth may ward off the anger of the Folk, provided it's taken from a grave no more than twenty-one years old. Provided, too, that the occupant of the grave was descended from, or married into, the family that established the churchyard.

I came in at an iron gate. In the middle of the churchyard was a fresh slab heading a slash of raw earth, now very muddy, as it was still raining. That would be Lord Merton, just recently buried. According to the inscription, very clean and crisp, His Lordship had been sixty-four years old.

I walked round the graveyard. There were old headstones, all older than twenty-one years; too old to help. Then a grave lying at a little distance from Lord Merton's. I pulled aside the ivy to read the stone, and there was the Lady Rona again.

THE LADY RONA. That was all it said, and as I let the ivy fall back into place, a dark cloud caught the corner of my eye. It came streaming from a circular shaft at the far end of the cemetery; and I thought at first it was smoke, very strange to see in the rainy air.

But no smoke ever made that faint fluttering. I spoke aloud. "Not smoke, bats!"

I'd heard of these shafts in the ground, opening directly into the Caverns and walled off for safety. The Folk were closer than I'd known, but if the bats could turn their backs on them, so could I. There was a last grave, tiny, tucked under the chapel eaves. The carved Saints set into the wall looked down on it with empty stone eyes. It, too, was covered with lichen and ivy, and here again there was no name, but an epitaph:

> *Unnamed from the darkness came.*
> *Unnamed to the darkness returned.*
> *Born and died: Midsummer Eve.*

Who was buried in these last two graves? If only they were Marblehaugh Park descendants, and not more than twenty-one years buried, the mold from their graves might serve me against the Folk.

I would have to ask Finian, barter away another Conviction.

It was time to tell Mrs. Bains I was well enough to join the family for supper.

Mrs. Bains has made me a suit! It is very fine, of watered gray silk, with embroidered bands on the breeches. There are seventeen buttons to the waistcoat, and each of them a pearl. Not that I care; I am no dandy like Sir Edward.

Sir Edward and Lady Alicia were glad I was well enough to come to supper for the first time, but Finian teased me about how handsome I looked.

"Don't mind him," said Lady Alicia, very handsome herself in claret silk over an embroidered underskirt. "Finian's still a little boy who likes to be out poking worms onto hooks and never washing his hands."

Supper was a waste of time; there was no chance to speak to Finian alone. The dining room was scarlet and gold, with yards of table bursting with candelabra. Identical footmen in striped livery and powdered hair served us. They must all be brothers to the Valet, or cousins at least, their lips all pursed like respectable prunes.

Old Francis was the only one who didn't match, now stumbling against a chair, now struggling with a platter of dumplings, now chilling me with his frozen eye.

I understood why Finian was so bored. It was all talk about the weather and the estate, and to an estate, weather is everything.

"Well, Corin," said Lady Alicia. "How do you like this rain of ours?"

"I like it very well," I said, which is perhaps the first true thing I've ever told her. I like rain and mist. I've never understood why people exclaim over bright skies and bushels of glaring sunshine.

"It will help our crops," said Sir Edward.

Then it was all crops until the end of dinner. Lady

Alicia asking questions of Sir Edward, trying very hard to learn about the estate, and Finian making faces at me, but I never laugh when I don't choose.

We retired to the Music Room after supper. From weather to crops to music; and still no chance to speak to Finian. The Music Room was small by Manor standards (not big enough to hold more than fifty elephants), and all white and gold, with huge marble fireplaces that yawned into the room with tongues of flame.

The music was not too bad, really.

Lady Alicia sat at a spinet in an alcove; Finian raised his little whistle. The room gradually reduced itself to a golden bubble, just big enough to hold a candle, Lady Alicia's shining hair, and Finian's big fingers dancing over a scrap of tin. The silver thread of Finian's whistle wove itself into a rainbow of arpeggios as Lady Alicia spiraled to the final chord. She kissed Finian's cheek before she left the alcove. She did love him best of all, anyone could see that.

"Look at Corin's eyes shining!" said Finian. He took Lady Alicia's place, perching his big body on the delicate stool. I stood beside him. We were private enough; Lady Alicia had moved three or four leagues away to stand before the fire.

"I owe you a Conviction," I said.

"I've been waiting for it."

"This must be your business," I said. "Discover what those around you love best. Then, if they forbid you from doing as you choose, you have a hold on them. You can threaten their dearest treasures."

"I don't think I'd be very good at that." Finian and I

were much of a height, now that he was seated. "Is that how you get what you like?"

"I'll tell you more in exchange for another Secret."

"Another Conviction?" He took off his spectacles and stared as though he could see better without them. There was a blue vein running from the corner of his eye into the bridge of his nose. You sometimes see it in babies. "Very well, what do you want to know?"

"Who is the Lady Rona?"

"Who was she, you mean. She was Lord Merton's first wife. She went mad, which I can understand, being married to him!"

"Did she die fewer than twenty-one years ago?" I said.

"Oh, yes," he said, "although she died young. Mrs. Bains says she'll never forget how Her Ladyship was terrified of the sea—screamed if she even looked at it—but otherwise never spoke a word."

"Poor Lady," I said.

"Poor Lady," said Finian. "Mrs. Bains says she used to walk round and round, her hair streaming all about. She says the Lady could glide through crowds of furniture and people with her eyes closed!"

Until then I'd felt a certain kinship with the solitary Lady Rona, set apart from everyone else, but here we parted ways. I could walk through nothingness and stumble every time.

"She'd spend hours in the Cellar, too," said Finian, "and never bring a candle."

"She must have had a candle!" I said.

"To hold off the Folk, you mean?" said Finian. "I have always wondered how she survived them."

I nodded, but there was more to it than that. Without a light, how could she have chiseled her name into the walls?

"I love to gossip with Mrs. Bains," said Finian. "I tell her she's my sweetheart, and she gossips all the more."

"I thought the *Windcuffer* was your sweetheart."

"I lie sometimes," he said. "You do as well, don't you, to get what you want?"

I had a very nasty feeling that Finian could see more without his spectacles than most people could who needed none.

Finian spoke over my silence. "I'll have my Conviction now."

"You must avenge yourself on people who mistreat you," I said. "You must destroy what they love." I thought of the Valet, of his love for himself, and how I'd squashed it.

"So bloodthirsty, Corin!" said Finian. "Perhaps I'm too weak for your Convictions." He unfolded his body from the stool. "There's Mrs. Bains with the cakes, and I've always been partial to pink icing."

"Wait!" I said. "I have another Conviction, and I need another Secret." I knew now that Lady Rona was a proper descendant of the owners of Marblehaugh Park, but what of the unnamed person beneath the tiny gravestone?

"But I can't digest your Convictions," said Finian. "Give me something gentler next time. Just remind me it's worth fighting for my dream of building ships and having a life with the sea."

Have I ever felt so dreadful in my life? So squirmy inside, so like an insect or a worm?

"Think on it, Corin. Come sailing with me and give me a new sort of Conviction then."

"I haven't time for sailing." The more time I spent in the Cellar, the more likely it was I'd catch the Folk in a moment of mischief and draw off their anger.

"But you want to know the Secret?" said Finian.

He knew I did. He had his own way of getting what he wanted. "Very well," I muttered. "I'll come sailing."

"Promise?"

"Promise." I offered my fingertip, so we could swear on blood, but he said he'd believe me without.

Why does he insist so on my promise? They are inconvenient things, promises. I rarely keep them, myself.

February 17

I didn't tell Mrs. Bains why I wanted the pins. No one saw me last night when I slipped off to the Cellar, hundreds of pins stuck crosswise in my clothes. No one, that is, except the mournful old dog, Taffy, who followed me to the Kitchens, where I filled a bucket with very fresh and bloody meat.

"It's not for you!" I shut the Cellar door in his face and heard him sink to the floor, wheezing like an ancient bellows.

The pins held the Folk off only a moment. Their cobwebbed energy paused, then struck. My bones echoed with their screams; the pins burned with cold.

There came a howling from the world above. I fastened on the sound to suspend myself above the tightening round my muscles, the cramping that pulled every nerve to the outside.

Think of nothing but the time, Corinna, the passing of the hours. A quarter past midnight. Twenty-three minutes past two. Eight minutes past three.

It was half past four when I opened my eyes. My cheek lay pressed to the floor. The pins were stuck into my flesh, and at all angles. I was twenty-five minutes picking them out.

As for the meat, the Folk had eaten it, every scrap. Only bones remained, and even those were marked with shapes that looked like nothing so much as a legion of large square teeth. The Folk in Rhysbridge were never so fiercely ravenous.

I came up the Cellar stairs into the smell of baking bread. I'd forgotten about the old dog, with his watery yellow eyes, who flapped his feeble tail at me. He hauled himself up from his station beneath the ever-burning candle.

"Go away!" Those blunted teeth were nothing to me now. I'd seen what real teeth could do. But Taffy's toenails clicked behind me, down the corridor, up the stairs. If I could, I'd turn him back with the power of The Last Word. I heard from the pattern of his toenails that he was winding up the treads, side to side, to soften the angle of his climb.

I stopped at a rattling from above. Old Francis, coming down with a coal scuttle.

He stopped too, and there we were, the three of us on the stairs: Taffy below, stiff and arthritic; Old Francis above, stiff and paralyzed; and me in the middle, stiff and silent. There was only the sound of Taffy wheezing.

"I heard the dogs howling," said Old Francis presently.

"Dogs will howl at anything." But it was too late for bluffing.

"I know how it is," he said. "They howl when the Folk scream. You tried the pins, I see. Try scissors, opened to a cross. It worked for me many times."

He bowed, then passed without another look. I will accept any advice he chooses to offer, but if he knows I need advice, he also knows I haven't the power of The Last Word. He'd best not tell anyone. My revenge would be swift and terrible.

I made sure I was the first one at breakfast. But instead of filling my Folk Bag, I found myself staring at the platters of bacon and poppy cakes, the bowls of sardines in oil, the tankards of honey ale. I peered into a chaffing dish. Steam rose from a mound of eggs in cream, misting the silver lid. It all of a sudden seemed terribly futile. I had lost control of the Folk. What was the point in saving anything for them?

I reached for the sardines. The smell raised a hungry sea beneath my tongue. I dropped them into my mouth, one by one, dunking bread in the oil to soften it, then catching up the last drops with my fingers. My hands still smell of fish.

And I am still famished.

6

Fastern's E'en to the *Tirls of March*

February 19—Fastern's E'en

The Folk have been quiet. Today they ate:

Two small lambs
One tub of butter
One vat of kidney stew.

I've taken to stringing an open scissors about my neck, as Old Francis suggested, where it hangs in a crude sign of the cross. I will save the churchyard mold for the next major feast day. The dark energy seeps out the Folk Door in the same way, and the Folk batter the lamb bones in the same way, but they've not yet again battered Corinna.

The old dog, Taffy, has joined me in the Cellar. Oh, the smell of him—a combination of unwashed fur and advanced age, rather like sharp cheese. He scratched so at the Cellar door I could not endure it. Neither could Cook, who opened the door and sent him down.

You have been forced upon me, Taffy, make no mistake about it. What gives you the confidence to rest your chin on my boot? Go away! Why do you wag your tail when I look at you? I cannot promise you will not be hurt. But the Folk are quiet, for now.

March 3

I am learning the ways of the Northern Isles. The Folk here grow very fierce during the Storms of the Equinox, which occur once in the autumn and once in the spring. The spring Storms are fewer than three weeks away. I must be prudent. These Folk have injured me more on one minor feast day and two very ordinary days than the Folk in Rhysbridge ever did in four entire years.

I must find out who's buried beneath that little headstone.

Finian made me promise to go sailing; perhaps then I could learn the secret. In Rhysbridge, after all, I used to haunt the market, picking up scraps of charms and spells. No, one cannot spend all one's time in the Cellar. One must be prudent.

March 7

I sit on the cliff top, looking at a jar of amber beads. Finian gave them to me this morning. The clean Cliffsend sun slices through, irradiating them with light. There must be dozens, each a key to an exquisite freedom, and Finian says I may have as many as I like!

I stepped outside this morning into shredded streamers of mist. Saturated air hung from my eyebrows, from the fine hairs on the back of my neck. I tumbled down the cliff path into the smell of tar. "What, no Folk Bag!" said Finian.

I tapped my forehead. "Everything I need is right here."

I did not like to think of losing the Bag overboard in a careless moment, and so I left it in the Cellar, where the Lady Rona will watch over it with her pleas for pity. It will be safe there.

"Perhaps," said Finian, "you can untangle this line with those little fingers of yours."

I have vowed never again to be anybody's drudge. But while we waited for the mist to burn off, it seemed foolish not to help Finian with his repairs on the *Windcuffer*. How different this was—even stirring the pitch!—from the work I'd left behind, the endless scrubbing and hauling and humiliations before I became a Folk Keeper. Finian spoke of replacing the floor with new mahogany boards shipped all the way from the Mainland. I will help him, with a hammer, even if it means losing two thumbs, or even three.

I could not, however, untangle the line.

The mist lifted itself gradually from my hair, and by the time we set sail in *The Lady Rona*, the day had turned brilliant. The air had a special dazzle, the clouds scrubbed very white, hung out to dry against a bowl of blue. *The Lady Rona*. Strange to name a boat for a lady who would have nothing to do with the sea.

Finian handed me a jar of amber beads. I tossed one in the sea. "For smooth sailing," I said as Finian cast off.

He smiled at me. "May the Sealfolk swim unharmed!"

My voice came as an echo. "May the Sealfolk swim unharmed!"

Finian peeled off his spectacles. "I don't need these out here. I'm good at distance. It's being closed up in that damnable Manor I hate, where I'm trapped, expected to learn the ways of a lord. Out here is the only place you can be free."

"For you, perhaps," I said. "For me, it's the Cellar."

"That's what the Lady Rona thought, too. But she was mad. Perhaps you've forgotten about this." Finian handed me the tiller and the sheet that walks the sail through the wind.

"I never forget." Then I, Corinna Stonewall, showed him how I could coax the wind to lean its powerful shoulder against our boat, and the sea needed no coaxing to lift us from below. Off skimmed *The Lady Rona* between the press of wind and water.

"And on your second time out!" said Finian.

"I told you, I don't forget."

We drew quickly away from the cliffs. Finian pointed out a thumbprint of civilization on the Cliffsend coast, not more than an hour's walk from the Manor. A tumble of slate-roofed cottages and a crazy-quilt cathedral, all red and yellow stone. "Firth Landing," he said. "You'll go there in August for the Harvest Fair."

"I can't leave my Cellar," I said.

"Everyone goes," said Finian.

But I am not everyone.

"You are stubborn, Corin." Finian shook his head. "So attached to that Cellar of yours you miss what's right before your nose. What would be so bad if you gave it up, became a gentleman?"

"Then," I said, "I'd be in the position of one Finian Hawthorne. *Sir* Finian Hawthorne."

"Didn't I say I'd box your ears if you call me *Sir*. Retract it now, and you shall be spared grievous bodily harm." As usual, Finian was half laughing, but this time, no more than half. I felt suddenly sorry for him. It is a peculiar feeling; I do not care for it.

"But I can't take it back," I said. "That *Sir* is attached to your name, and to you. It means that the mistress of Marblehaugh Park may forbid you to do as you like with your life. Sir Edward, too."

"You are difficult to argue with, Corin, but still I say you shall come to the Harvest Fair."

"Still I say I will not!"

Finian laughed suddenly. "You are just like your name, stubborn, a stone wall."

It is true, and not merely by chance. I was named from the scrap of paper found upon me as an infant. *Corinna*, it said, but gave no second name. *Stonewall* was given me one long-ago day, in one of those endless foundling homes, when I refused to boil the soiled linens. Why should I—I who wanted so much to learn to read and write? But that privilege was granted only the most promising boys.

The Matron there called me *stubborn!* and whipped me with a leather strap, and ever after I was known as Corinna Stonewall.

"What are you thinking?" said Finian.

I couldn't tell him. Finian wouldn't like the way I avenged myself for that whipping . . . Now Corinna, you must not fall into the trap of caring what Finian likes, or anybody else.

"I have a Conviction for you," I said at last.

"You first, this time," said Finian. "I have to know it's worth a Secret."

I was silent a long time.

"You can trust me. Fair's fair. Until now I've been giving away my Secrets for free."

I'd worked out my Conviction, but the words were hard to say. It was too soft for my taste; it wanted backbone. "I sat on the cliffs last night. The tide was low and steam rose from the water."

"Sea smoke," said Finian.

"The water seemed suddenly marvelous, now it can be smoke, now ice, now liquid. Nothing lost, only rearranged." I'd thought of how—all unknowing—I'd imitated it, turning Corinna into Corin, nothing lost, just a little surface rearrangement.

"I plucked my Conviction for you from the sea. Do as the water does. Hide what you're doing. Hide even what you are. Then no one can stop you."

"Are you speaking of your own secrets?" said Finian.

"I don't have any secrets!"

"Of course not," said Finian. I hate it when he speaks so gently. A person might turn to mush inside and pour away. But not I, not Corinna Stonewall.

"My Conviction, is it acceptable?"

"It is a good Conviction," said Finian. "The Secret is yours."

"Who is buried under the headstone under the chapel eaves?"

"Still looking for friends in the churchyard?" said Finian. "That was the Lady Rona's child."

"A child! What happened?"

Finian shrugged. "Babies die, mothers die, and often in childbed, which was the case here."

"But there's no name."

"It died unbaptized," said Finian, "which is why the baby's buried apart from the mother, by the chapel. The vicar hoped the rain falling from the eaves onto the grave might turn holy enough to baptize the baby instead."

And so now I have a jar of amber beads, and my Secret, too. The baby was also a descendant of the owners of Marblehaugh Park, and I will take earth from its grave and try it against the Folk. But what if it fails to protect me? Or what if I fail to protect the estate? For the first time, I am afraid.

March 15—Tirls of March

I have been pinched, nothing worse.

The Folk have eaten:

> Five dozen salted kippers
> Two crates of dried beef.

And what has Corinna eaten?

I woke last night, famished. I had been dreaming of water shot with silver bodies. I pulled on my clothes as though in a dream, tiptoed down the marble stairs, and across the sodden grass.

It was high tide, and waves lapped at the edge of the beach. I plunged my hand into the beating water, snatched at a bright streak. The fish thrashed between my fingers. I did not hesitate. I broke its neck, and before its jellied eye grew dim, I bit into the sweet and living flesh.

7

Storms of the Equinox Through *Egg Sunday* (and Other Matters I'd Rather Not Discuss)

March 21—The Spring Equinox

I felt the Storms coming this morning, a gathering of tension, the air winding itself up for a secret celebration. The petrels skimmed the water in black clouds, harbingers of those to come.

It hit us tonight at supper. A wave of water rattled the glass as lightning staggered from the skies. It seemed alive, the storm, speaking with a voice of its own. I could love this fearsome weather if the Folk did not also grow fierce.

"It's started again," said Lady Alicia.

"My tender nerves!" cried Finian, clasping his hands to his breast. "Already I can't stand it."

"Don't be silly," said Sir Edward.

"There's nothing silly about the Storms," said Finian,

but he was speaking to me rather than to Sir Edward. "Don't go out, Corin. The cottagers tether their hens against the wind. You're such a little thing; we should tether you as well."

"Isn't he a bit bigger?" said Lady Alicia. "I'd swear he's grown since he first came."

"Boys will grow," said Sir Edward, shrugging. "What's your sacrifice to be, Corin?"

"Sacrifice?"

"Sacrifice," he said, drumming his fingers on the table. "Only a live sacrifice will do for the Folk during the Storms."

"The Folk don't eat living creatures!"

"And you call yourself a Folk Keeper!" Sir Edward slapped his palm on the table. "Maybe those pallid creatures you call the Folk in Rhysbridge are contented with a few crumbs. But not the Folk of Marblehaugh Park!"

"I know the Folk." But did I know them well enough? Bribing a lad or two for information, listening in on conversations of charms and spells. What had I missed, picking up scraps of knowledge about the Folk as I had?

Sir Edward echoed my thoughts. "You know everything about the Folk, do you? After caring for a mere hundred households in Rhysbridge!" He peeled his hand from the table. The moist outline of his palm melted from the polished wood.

"One hundred twenty-eight households," I said.

"An estate is a far greater thing than a handful of city tradesmen and their scrawny chickens. Think what damage the Folk could do to us—blight our spring crop; raise blisters on the pigs; sour the wine we've bottled for the Harvest Fair."

Sir Edward knew nothing of the Folk. "They can't sour the wine," I said. "It's neither meat nor egg nor . . ."

"Before that happens," said Sir Edward, "I'll find myself another Folk Keeper." Lightning flashed through the window and wrapped itself around his head.

Old Francis stood behind me. "I've had enough," I said. "You may take my plate."

That is all I said. It is best not to let your enemy know your anger. Vengeance, my mind was full of it. Sir Edward loved the estate best of all, but I could not destroy that. My place depended on it.

I trailed after the others to the Music Room, stretching my lips agreeably as they laughed at the hounds, at fierce Liquorice, so terrified of the Storms he tried to squeeze beneath a sofa. He fit only up to his red ears, and there he lay, sides heaving, pretending all of him was hidden.

Taffy was undisturbed by the thunder. I felt rather smug (he belongs to me more than anyone, following me everywhere as he does) until I realized he is so deaf he doesn't hear it much.

The Storms brought out the worst in everyone, and a good thing too, for it was Finian, gibing slyly at Sir Edward, who found my revenge for me.

"Just the right night for a moonlight sail, eh, Corin?" he said, leaning over the dessert tray and arranging twenty or thirty cakes on his hand.

"Won't you ever stop this useless playing around with boats!" said Sir Edward.

"That's all it is," said Finian gently, but he was watching Sir Edward closely. "Just playing."

"Why couldn't you play about with something more fitting?" Lightning struck, illuminating the world fiercely and briefly, catching every leaf and blade of grass in its white eye. "Your stepfather would have been proud to see you add a trophy to our collection. Both he and I have our prizes. Mine, that great pelt from the black jungle beast. Hartley, that silvery one."

Sir Edward was speaking almost calmly now, his irritation draining away into small talk. "Hartley took a number of silvery ones over the years, mostly smaller, as I recall. I wonder what became of them?"

Finian threw a coal on the fire. "How thoughtless of His Lordship to marry my mother."

He spoke lightly, but a thread of malice ran beneath his voice, puckering it slightly in hidden places. "Neither she nor I knows how to run the estate, which it seems you must do by tacking dead things to the walls. A pity we ousted you from your inheritance, Edward. I know you were counting on it."

Sir Edward sprang to his feet, lithe and muscular as a cat—finicky as one, too, in his black and white satin. Finian shook the cakes from his hand and very calmly took off his spectacles.

The bear against the cat. I knew which of them would win.

"For shame, gentlemen!" cried Lady Alicia, spoiling all the fun. Finian bowed coldly to Sir Edward, and I left without a word. I had waited too long to tend the Folk. My revenge would have to wait.

I slipped past Cook in the Kitchens, who was fighting a lump of dough and raging at the wind. "Will it never be still!"

I threaded myself through the vegetable gardens and

the tangle of out-buildings, hiding from the weather behind the stables, the brewery, the dairy. But on the exposed seaward side, the wind was a fierce thing, almost alive. It flattened me against the wall with an invisible thumb, but I beat at it with my head and shoulders until it gave way. Nothing was going to keep me from the churchyard, and the wind at last understood.

The latch on the churchyard gate stuck fast. My hands do not grow stiff with cold, but they are clumsy. I finally gave up and scaled the fence, ripping my jacket on a picket. The fingers of the storm scribbled a vast wild portrait on the sky, while through a window, a single candle burned. It was Finian, his hair very red in the glow.

I scooped a handful of wet earth from His Lordship's grave. "To ward off the Folk." The Lady Rona's grave was not so easy, as the grasses and lichens wove the mold fast into itself. But if the wind couldn't turn me aside, neither could mere grass. I scrabbled about and gathered another handful of earth, much of it under my fingernails.

Last, to the tiny headstone. I felt briefly sorry for the baby, set apart to receive the drippings of water from the chapel eaves. But maybe she's like me: I don't mind a little wet.

Before I left, I stood by the stone wall that surrounds the shaft opening into the Caverns. Eight feet around perhaps, and tall as I am. I tried to toss my words inside, where they might fall into the ears of the Folk—if they have ears.

"I'm ready for you!"

But I wasn't sure.

I was less sure still when I sat in the Cellar, concentric rings of salt, bread, and churchyard mold rippling out around me. I felt the hum of energy behind the Door, closed my eyes, and snuffed the candle.

The Folk first crackled over the roasted lambs—seven of them!—silently picking them clean, then absorbed the butter and the sardines. Only then did they turn their hollow energy my way.

When was it they paused? At the ring of churchyard mold? At the crosswise scissors? I only know that bare seconds before they would have touched me, the energy sank back into itself and retreated.

Sir Edward was wrong: The Folk are mild as lambs during the Storms.

March 22

I was full of a strange energy when I left the Cellar, even growing two shadows as I passed between the double rows of candles that lined the corridors. All the sconces were lit on this stormy night. The shadows shrank again into my heels when I stepped into the Trophy Room. There was just enough light to see a dozen wet noses and twice as many glistening eyes turned my way.

The hounds yawned and stretched to show their contempt. Liquorice and Honeycomb paced beside me as I fetched a step stool. "Puppies!" I said scornfully, just to remind them of how they'd hidden so shamefully from the thunder.

The jungle beast's skin was heavier than I'd expected. It toppled me off the stool and onto the bony part of my hip. "At it, lads!" I heaved it as best I could.

Taffy did not stir, but the others leapt upon the skin. I'd been afraid they might begin that inhuman baying of theirs, but they were silent. Terribly silent. I waited until the skin was savaged beyond recognition.

Will you be proud, Sir Edward, proud of your prize trophy now? It is a measure of your power, just as my position of Folk Keeper is a measure of mine. Never threaten my power, for then I will threaten yours.

By twenty-six minutes past three in the morning, my vengeance was complete.

By ten minutes to seven, all the dogs were in disgrace. They slunk about, red ears pinned to their heads, yellow eyes downcast. Sir Edward spoke of it calmly enough at breakfast. Who could understand it? he asked. He seemed calm, I say, but there was a little scar I'd not noticed before, almost hidden by his eyebrow, which turned livid when he spoke.

"If anything," said Sir Edward, "I wish they'd destroyed the silvery skin instead. It looks to be ruined in any event, as it is somehow stretching."

Then again and again, "Why did the hounds do it? Why?"

Lady Alicia said that the Storms must have driven them wild, and so did Mrs. Bains and even the Valet. But Finian did not speak. He removed his spectacles and pinched the bridge of his nose as he does when he's tired, then looked so purposefully away from me that my heart jumped. He knew!

I'm back in the Cellar now, inside my triple-layered protection, but not protected from a nasty certainty. He knows. Finian knows.

And what if he does? He hasn't given me away; he won't do so, I think. What more do I care about? I think only of Cook's promise to save me a platter of sardines, dried and salted. They are so fragile even I can eat them, bones and all. Why have I grown ravenous at Marblehaugh Park? I cannot wait to feel the crunch of bones between my teeth.

April 1—All Fools' Day

Mrs. Bains says the Folk are very well, and quiet. They have consumed:

> Six brace of quail
> A shoulder of pork
> Five chickens.

The Storms are over, but the memory of them remains. The wind's voice is rough, tired from screaming.

I never screamed. What a pity that my writing hand is free from hurt, so I must record what happened the second night of the Storms.

The Folk didn't touch me with a touch that is physical, but I have the bruises still. They sank beneath my skin, ripping through tissue and fiber into the heart of my bones. It hurt red-hot for what seemed a long time, then faded into a slow numbness, which faded into a merciful feeling of no feeling at all.

It seemed merciful, but it was not. It was the ruinous paralysis from which some never recover. I realized it only when Finian gathered me from the Cellar floor. He was the only one brave enough to charge down the stairs when all at once the dogs set to howling. There was the warmth of my right side against him, the beating of his heart against my ear, and on the other side—nothing. No press of circling arms, no warmth.

Sir Edward has explained to everybody's satisfaction how I could have the power of The Last Word and still be injured. (Certainly to Lady Alicia's satisfaction, who thinks him the Saint of All Knowledge.) It is convenient to be able to say that without a sacrifice, the Folk grow so wild during the Storms they all but overwhelm The Last Word.

It is less convenient that I cannot believe it. Why didn't the Folk hurt me as badly as Old Francis? Kill me, even? I shall recover as Old Francis never did.

Saints be praised that the Folk do not again grow so fierce until the Feast of the Keeper, in July. Between now and then I must find new protection.

April 12—Egg Sunday

I should report on the Folk on this feast day, but I'd rather report on myself.

Oh, very well: The Folk have been quiet. They have consumed:

> Three dozen buckets of first milk
> Two hundred and seven eggs, leaving no
>   shells
> A side of beef.

Mrs. Bains insists I am too ill to leave the Manor. But I am quite recovered. Best not tell her I slipped out this morning, hid myself among the drifting fog-wraiths all the way to the cliffs.

The beach was littered with debris: dead fish and birds, feathers, driftwood (driftwood, on this treeless island!). The sun shone behind the mist like a full moon. Seagulls stood in tidy rows, still exchanging stories about the storm.

It was low tide and at the edge of the beach was a five-foot drop to a scatter of rocks. The tide pools were overflowing with water, bursting with life. Beneath the tenacious algae, dozens of happy creatures were doubtless going about their daily business.

Life, life. I smelled it all around. The green sea, bursting with life, from the sea urchins amongst the rocks below to the barnacles and seaweed creeping up the pilings of the pier. The poets always sing of bright blue water, but I don't care for it. Blue is nothing; blue has only itself to reflect.

All the others in the Manor will be stuffing themselves with eggs on this Sunday. But not I.

I leaned off the pier, casting glances over my shoulder even as my hand darted into the water. Mrs. Bains wants to feed me, but she cannot know what I really want. Flesh, sweet and salty, bursting with life. I threw the entrails to the birds, the skeletons to the sea.

April 17—Levy Day

The Folk have eaten:

>Two roast ribs
>
>Five rounds of cheese
>
>A barrel of smoked haddock.

I do not regret destroying Sir Edward's prize trophy. I do regret that Finian suspects me. I should have known never to reveal any of my true Convictions. And for what? The Secrets were no good. The churchyard mold failed to work against the Folk. What shall I do come July, during the Feast of the Keeper, when the Folk next grow wild?

8

Beltane Through *Midsummer*

May 1—Beltane

Old Francis has disappeared.

He vanished during the Storms of the Equinox, but I learned of it only this morning, when the chapel bells shook us all out of bed and into the meadow behind the Manor. It was lovely in the early light, gathering violets and marsh marigolds for the May Day garlands. Clouds of sheep floated in distant fields, and dandelions lay scattered like spots of sunshine.

Lady Alicia made five garlands, and Finian made three. His big fingers are remarkably nimble. Sir Edward gave a little boy a copper to gather flowers for him, but then even he spread his elegant coattails in the grass and constructed his garlands with the deliberate care he devotes to all affairs of the Manor.

I managed one garland, which might, with luck, fit a head shaped like a triangle.

"Of all the feast days," said Lady Alicia, plucking at the grass, "Old Francis loved May Day best." She brought her palm level with her face, then blew the grass into the wind. "These are easy days, he always said. Easy for a Folk Keeper."

Old Francis? I looked about. He was nowhere among the knots of Manor servants laughing and gathering flowers.

Finian set a garland on my head. "You'll not see him here. No one's seen him since the Storms."

I hadn't thought of him for weeks.

Easy days for a Folk Keeper. Yes, the Folk are quiet now a long while, today eating only a hogshead of boiled pig knuckles. The May Day garlands are scattered in a circle round the Manor, restricting the power of the Folk to the Caverns. Likewise, during the Masquerade Ball on Midsummer Eve, the Manor will be circled with a ring of burning torches. We do not celebrate Midsummer Eve on the Mainland, but Mrs. Bains assures me this fiery ring will keep the Folk subdued.

These have indeed been easy days. I've been busy with Finian, putting the final touches on the *Windcuffer*. We've been breaking in her new set of sails, puttying her cracks and seams with lead-and-linseed oil, and painting her properly, with many thin coats. She dried slowly, gleaming in the spring sun.

The *Windcuffer* has come alive, just as everything in Cliffsend has sprung suddenly to life. Banks of buttercups shine everywhere, and the hyacinths are making a great show of themselves, each of their leaves carefully combed and curled.

Everything's come to life, and all this while I never noticed Old Francis was gone. I wish I'd noticed earlier. Then I'd never have worried he'd tell my secret, reveal I don't have the power of The Last Word. He can't tell anyone, now.

June 16—Feast of Saint Jerud, Who Throttled a Sea Serpent

It has taken the Folk all day to eat a mere dozen cheeses, but I rose for breakfast at dawn. There was just a tiny brightening to the east, like the pinkish-gray luster in the lining of a shell. The fish were easy marks, hovering at the surface during their great nightly grazing. I struck again and again.

By the time Finian arrived, I was bursting with Convictions.

I told him the sun shines on the seafloor in a grillwork of fractured light.

I told him the sky is delicately cobwebbed with clouds, that gulls fly over the water like scattered confetti.

"I like these new Convictions," he said. "How wonderfully you Folk Keepers are schooled. You find the right words to describe the Folk, and everything else, too."

But no one schooled me. I had to school myself.

I told Finian he owes me two Secrets.

When I read this over, I realize how different I sound from the old Corinna. I'm not turning into a sentimental girl, am I? Swooning over the sunset and dabbing lavender water on my wrists? I must be alert to signs of encroaching softness. I need a new morning routine:

75

clean teeth, wash face, check heart for signs of dry rot. Replace it with good mahogany planking, as we did the *Windcuffer*. It'll last a long time.

June 21—Midsummer Eve

It is half past ten, and there's still an underglow to the sky. The Cliffsenders boast that on Midsummer midnight you can read without a candle, or play a game of ball, if the ball is white.

I sit on the cliffs, but even here I am not far enough removed from the Midsummer festivities. Why do people do it, having guests to stay for a whole week? First you have to endure the washing of draperies and airing of beds and beating of carpets (all of which had seemed more than clean enough to me). Then you have to endure the hideous chatter of the ladies and gentlemen and their maids and valets; and even beg Cook for a barrel of dried beef for the Folk on this feast day.

You can never get far enough away. Sounds from the Masquerade Ball drift across the lawn. Arching streamers of violin music, the rumble of distant talking and laughter, a happy scream. Someone won at cards, or had her dress trod on, or was kissed!

I stood out from the others earlier tonight when I entered the Ballroom in my Samson costume. Yes, I dressed as Samson, he of the long hair. We are a little alike, he and I, for our hair sets us apart. His gave him strength, and mine—well, it is inconvenient that it grows two inches each night, but it is one of my secret powers. Not for anything would I give it up.

My white tunic was very plain among the jesters and

their bells, the wizards and their staffs, the fairies and their jewels, fragile shoulders rising from beds of ribbon and gauze. But my costume hid more secrets than theirs. So did my hair, which I've grown to my chin and colored with a walnut stain. I seem to be wearing a wig. No one would guess it's mine. I like to be fooling them all.

Midsummer Eve is my birthday, and there is one disappointment that has come with turning sixteen. I seem to be starting to grow. I can wear the tunic and still be thought a boy, but not for long, perhaps. Not for long.

I slipped round the edges of the crowd, avoiding the crystal chandeliers, whose hundreds of candles were already dripping hot wax. Poor Mrs. Bains. I knew her armies had spent hours polishing the Ballroom floor with beeswax and cleaning the chandeliers until each crystal was beautifully radiant.

A footman handed me a glass. Tiny lines of bubbles streamed through pale liquid. The fiddle cried out in a language that everyone but I understood. Like pieces of a kaleidoscope, the ladies and gentlemen fell into patterns of color on the Ballroom floor.

I slipped out the French doors; dancing is not for me. The indoors and out-of-doors were all mixed together. Armfuls of ivory roses bloomed everywhere inside the Manor; outside, an immense Oriental carpet suffocated the lawn—or so I heard the gardeners complain. On it stood a long buffet table, at which Mrs. Bains was counting bottles of champagne in a hollow ice-swan.

I stood on the lawn, between two worlds, watching the dance. Behind me, a couple of gardener lads argued about how to lay the Midsummer bonfire. Before me, the squares in the Ballroom fragmented, the ladies and gentlemen flowing into separate lines, then swirling themselves together with hooked elbows and clasped hands. It is traditional for the host and hostess to dress only as themselves: Sir Edward, never deviating from his black and white, Lady Alicia in rubies and gold satin.

Behind me, the gardener lads stood on step stools, lighting lanterns in globes of silver paper. Before me appeared Finian, a neat and careful dancer, his red cap bobbing above the others.

Now Finian, that wasn't a very good idea, was it? To dress as a Cliffsend fisherman! It will cast your mother into melancholy; it will irritate Sir Edward, who like his cousin, Lord Merton, wants to mold you into a copy of himself.

Behind me, the voices of the gardener lads faded away. Before me, the fisherman danced with a young lady dressed as the Tragic Queen, the one who wanted always to be eating cake. What can she be thinking? Even if I were still Corinna, and even if I had golden hair and liked to dress in spangled gauze, I'd never masquerade as someone who let them chop off her head.

Before me, the dancers relaxed into a crowd again. Finian handed a glass to his spangled partner.

I took a sip from my own. It was cold, and not very sweet.

Then Finian raised his glass.

Why can I not forget the picture he made, a mountain of white canvas, pale liquid glowing against bronzed skin?

I left the lawn then for the cliffs, and here I am, all my earlier fizz evaporated. I just had another sip. The champagne is warm and flat. My first champagne, and on my sixteenth birthday, too. It is not as I imagined.

Taffy lies beside me, keeping me company. He is arthritic and I am stiff, and neither of us is much for dancing and crowds.

There is a lump of desolation beneath the bony dip at my throat. It is no bigger than a coin, this spot, a peculiarly small place to hold so large a feeling. I try to shove it to some deeper region, but there it sticks, a fragile skin-thickness from the outside world.

Taffy rests his nose on my foot and sighs.

It's almost midnight. The dancers have spilled onto the lawn. I must join them now; it's time to light the bonfire. And then I'll go back to being the Folk Keeper of Marblehaugh Park. That is what I am, and I can't pretend to be Samson or anyone else.

9

Midsummer Midnight Through *Midsummer Dawn*

June 22

It is the gloves I remember best, elegant gloves of all colors, scattered on the ground. What a strange tumbled garden of lilac, primrose, and jonquil. And I remember, too, the naked, glittering fingers wrapped around unlit torches.

"Folk for the darkness!" cried Sir Edward, approaching the unlit bonfire with a burning taper. "Humans for the light!"

"Folk for the darkness!" echoed the crowd. "Humans for the light!" The skeleton pile of sticks burst into flame. "Ah!" The crowd fluttered around like moths.

Sir Edward again. "The first light goes to Lady Alicia!"

Again, the echo. "The first light . . . Lady Alicia!"

Someone pressed a torch into my hand, but I am no moth and stood back. Lady Alicia touched her torch to the bonfire. She seemed more fire than flesh as she broke off from the crowd, a torch-star floating round the Manor. One by one, the jesters, queens, and wizards dipped their torches in the flames and fell into a blazing orbit behind her.

I hung back until only Sir Edward and I stood before the fire. "Off you go, little Samson, and don't you fall."

That was just like Sir Edward, attending always to the business of the estate, organizing a mass of fire into a tight ring around the Manor in order to trap the mischief of the Folk in the Caverns.

I dipped my torch into the flames. "Do not fall!" I told myself, for any break diminishes the circle's power, and I joined the fiery constellation.

I usually despise crowds, all that senseless jostle and laughter, but now there was only the rustle of silk, the whisper of velvet. How could it be that I didn't even stumble? I flowed into that silent, blazing stream, running faster, now faster still—me, the slow after-thought of a star!

The crowd was dissolving into shrieks and laughter when I rounded the last wing of the Manor. Sir Edward and I stood a little apart from the others, watching them toss their torches into the flames; and when the clamor had organized itself into a chant, he tapped my shoulder and said, "They're calling for you."

"For me?" The words came clear, but not their meaning. *Jump!* A great shout. *The Folk Keeper shall jump!*

"What does it mean?" I cried as the crowd split from

itself, forming a long, snaking path to the fire. "What do they want!"

"You must leap the bonfire," said Sir Edward. "The Folk Keeper always goes first."

"Me?" They wanted me to run down the path they'd made and jump the flames? "I am too clumsy."

"It makes the strongest charm against the Folk," said Sir Edward. "The Folk Keeper must go first."

The crowd had found out my name. *Jump, Corin! Jump!*

"I've heard of no such thing," I said. But I didn't add it was most likely because Midsummer is not celebrated on the Mainland.

"It is time," said Sir Edward.

His hand was very tight on my elbow. Sir Edward, implacable about matters concerning the estate, steering me rather roughly to the head of the path.

The fire burned bright and hungry, licking its lips with a yellow tongue. "I shall fall into the flames," I said. Why did they keep feeding it old torches and armfuls of heather? "Even if I do not die, I shall be useless as your Folk Keeper."

"Then we shall find another." Sir Edward smiled to take the edge off his words, but he meant it, I could tell. I did not like him any the worse. You have to be ruthless to care for what you love.

Jump, Corin! Jump! The Folk Keeper shall jump!

I wrested my elbow from Sir Edward's grip, but he swung me back, lifting me half from my feet. A jeweled button raked my cheek. My breathing was trapped in a bubble of pressure. My arms were trapped, I had only my teeth. I snapped out, they sank into something soft. And then there was air and solid ground and the metallic taste of blood.

Most people would have cried out, but there was silence first, then Sir Edward saying, "That costume cannot disguise what you really are."

I had not thought it possible to be so afraid. My hair—could he tell it wasn't a wig? But a pair of canvas shoes moved into my ant's-eye view through the grass. He meant Finian, the fisherman.

"You know I love to argue with you, Edward." Finian lifted me from the ground and set me on my feet as though I were an egg. "But let's leave my costume for another day. I don't like these rough games with our little Folk Keeper."

"A true Folk Keeper," said Sir Edward, "would not hesitate to jump the flames."

The Folk Keeper shall jump!

Finian held out his hand. "I carried you from the Cellar the night the Storms began. You've grown a bit since, but no matter. I can surely help you over the flames."

"The Folk Keeper must go first," said Sir Edward.

"I promise," said Finian. "Our Folk Keeper shall be first over the flames. And Samson, I promise you'll clear the flames, although you must land on your own feet. I'll carry that damned inconvenient Folk Bag for you."

I yielded it up; I had no choice it seemed. Then, as we started down the path, Finian squeezed my elbow. "Ready?"

"No!" I said, and broke grudgingly into a run.

What Midsummer magic made my feet so sure and

fast tonight? I was an arrow, pulsing down the path, sprinting ahead of Finian, suddenly sure I did not need his help.

How did my feet know just when to gather speed, just when to spring? How did they clear the flames so neatly? I barely felt the heat before I stood on the other side.

Finian shall jump! Jump, Finian! Jump!

Finian landed lightly beside me. "You didn't need my help!"

I shrugged. Who could understand it. "You lost your cap."

"Now will Edward like my costume?" said Finian.

Andrew shall jump! Jump, Andrew! Jump!

Short plump legs churred down the lane. The crowd gasped when Sir Andrew landed on a burning log, then laughed.

"Is that how they do it on the Mainland, Andy!" someone shouted. And stout, good-natured Sir Andrew waved his smoldering shoe like a trophy. "I can't jump as their Folk Keeper does!"

Jump, Philip! Jump!

Sir Edward jumped last, a shimmer of white silk and diamond buttons. He would never lose a shoe to the fire, or a cap.

The first peat! cried a voice, and then a score of others. *Finian shall throw the first peat!*

Sir Edward handed Finian a brick of peat, then after a moment's hesitation, one to me. From the web of skin beside his thumb, shone the red moon of my teeth.

"You too, Corin," he said. "Throw a peat on the fire and see who your future wife will be."

"My wife?"

Finian shall throw the first peat!

It was laughing Sir Andrew of the smoldering shoe who finally explained it to me. Each unmarried person holds a half-burned brick of peat against his heart for no fewer than seven minutes. "When you break it in two, Corin, the color of the strands that hold the peat together will match the hair of the lucky lady you are to marry."

The crowd again. *Finian shall throw the first peat!* Sir Andrew glanced at the Tragic Queen with the golden hair and nudged me with his elbow. "We shall have some fun now." He raised his voice. "Will you find gold in there, Finian?"

There were shouts and cheers. The Tragic Queen blushed, and Finian said, "Do shut up!"

We all did shut up after we'd thrown our peat on the fire, watching it burn, taking care not to confuse our particular square with another's. Behind me Sir Edward whispered, "What if the strands in yours are black?"

Someone laughed nervously, and I had to glance round to see it was Lady Alicia. It was most unlike her. She was blushing, too.

Amiable Sir Andrew retrieved my peat for me. "Here you are, Samson. I hope the girl's a beauty, though you'll have to wait a few years."

It is lovely to hold a brick of warm peat to your breast. Who would have thought so? Your heart beats against it; you grow tranquil; your heart slows, thuds against warmth; the fibers of the peat glow against your skin, grow around your heart. The crowd grew calmer still, all of us just breathing and beating.

Sir Edward moved first, breaking his peat and peering into its heart. By the time Mrs. Bains began to set up for Midsummer breakfast on the lawn, the crowd had again grown shrill and giddy, teasing each other to say what color strands they'd found. The Tragic Queen shook her head and wouldn't say.

Sir Edward smiled at Lady Alicia. "Chestnut."

"Fair." Lady Alicia shrugged, mostly with her eyebrows. "My late husband was fair. Perhaps that means I shan't remarry."

Everyone looked at Finian. "I will never tell."

Sir Andrew asked me, but I'd put my peat in my Folk Bag without looking.

"Samson doesn't care for marriage," he said.

"No, I will never marry."

I slipped away, back to the cliffs where I have spent so much of this Midsummer Eve. I do not belong in that crowd of people looking for love. The sky is beginning to glow with its own inner light, and soon I will set off to collect Saint-John's-Wort. I cannot eavesdrop at the Rhysbridge market, but Mrs. Bains is almost as useful. She says that if you gather the herb exactly at Midsummer dawn, it may protect you against the Folk, who will soon again grow wild.

June 22

The evening sun hangs in my bedchamber mirror, setting the room on fire. Everything seems to have been on fire, from the torches tossing their reflection into dark windows, to the flames licking at Sir Andrew's shoe, to the bricks of smoking peat.

An evening all of fire, then all of water.

How lucky that the new, nimble Corinna stayed with

me all that short Midsummer night. Lucky, too, I hadn't yet left my cliff-top perch when the shouting began.

Two figures, white canvas and black satin, stood not two hundred feet away. How close they were to the edge of the cliff! I leapt to my feet just as the big one, in white, staggered backward and disappeared.

Time slowed down while I sped up. Now only five seconds had passed, now only twelve, but I seemed a long time running. Seventeen seconds, Sir Edward waving me back. "Run for help! I'll go in after him."

But I was a small tidal wave, boiling along the cliffs, blasting Sir Edward aside and peering over. The sea had swallowed Finian whole; there was not a bulge or seam to show where it had taken him in. I thought more of the plunge into the sea, fifteen feet down, than of how little I swim. When do I jump? Now? Now?

And oddly, it was the crowd's voice inside my head that helped me most. *The Folk Keeper shall jump!*

"I won't," I cried, and jumped.

Fifteen feet. It is nothing. I did not shatter against the water; I did not drown.

I was reborn.

I was born in reverse, exploded from one medium into another, from air into liquid, from dawn into darkness; and all around there was the singing of the sea.

I closed my ears—I can close my ears!—and against all proper instinct, squeezed my lungs empty of air. There came a slowing of the world—no, not of the world. A slowing of Corinna. A slowing into new life, not into drowning and death. I was suspended underwater yet needed no air, my heart beating to the slow, rhythmic pulse of underwater life.

The scratch from Sir Edward's button stung my cheek. There was a wild joy in that, and a joy, too, in releasing the burden of my own weight, exchanging thin air for this dense world.

I glanced everywhere, looking for a length of white canvas. But eyes are made to work with light; they're all but useless deep in the sea.

All this, which takes so long to explain, happened only in mental time. But real-world seconds started to tick away when I turned my head with its useless eyes, looking, looking, my hair following the motion of my head through water, and then . . .

You cannot be surprised underwater in the ways you are on land. You cannot gasp; you cannot stagger back. You observe calmly as your hair—well, I can only say that my hair opened a door into another dimension. It caught at the shape of a new world. Gone were all the hard edges, the corners, the troubling shifts of light and dark.

I saw a fish flicker behind me. I didn't see it with my eyes; rather, it sent a wave-image of itself, which I captured with my hair. I saw a ripple in the current, so tiny it might have been an echo of itself, shivering through liquid jade.

I made my own ripples, which bounced off the landscape and traveled back to me, explorers returning with maps of new territories. There were maps of scuttling crabs, maps of boulders, half as high as me. But where was the map of white canvas, which unlike the rest of the landscape, needed to breathe? I cast myself here—nothing. There—nothing.

Nothing.

Nothing.

There! A wave-picture describing not only Finian's shape, but also his composition. Mostly liquid, save for a pocket watch in his waistcoat, and in his jacket pocket the lacy outline of a key.

My hands were caught by old habits, still reaching ahead, grasping at handfuls of water, not believing my hair alone could guide me through the dark. They groped along invisible walls, utterly useless until they closed first on a rough sleeve, then on a head of hair. It took only one strong push off the seafloor.

Thank the Saints for water, dense almost as a large and heavy man, helping Finian to the surface.

I swear I've never breathed before. Air exploded into my lungs, into depths never before used. And as though I were hearing music, my hair rose, making an echo space above my scalp, filling with bubbles of air. I was marvelously buoyant. I was foam on the sea, wafting Finian to shore. I was a bubble, holding up the world.

My heart jumped from its deep-sea calm. I was re-inhabiting my land-body, or maybe it was re-inhabiting me. My ears opened of themselves to an assault of voices, jarring after that great silence. The babble screeched to a crescendo, now sorting itself into words.

"Corin! Corin!" Everyone calling my name, and then Sir Edward's voice above the rest. "Over here, lad!"

We'd drifted north and surfaced at the beach. The tide was flowing, water lapped almost at the edge. Long arms reached down, a hand heavy with rings grasped Finian and reeled him up. Another hand reached for me, but I sank below the surface, not yet ready to return to the world of laughter and tears and smoldering peat. The rock face was alive with tiny delicate branches. I'd known the barnacles only as hard conical shells, but underwater they reached with feathery legs to sweep the sea.

"Corin! Corin!" The voices came to me underwater. I closed my ears—extraordinary, I can truly close my ears. The voices vanished. But what if there were news of Finian? I rose to the surface.

"Your hand, Corin!" My buoyant sea-body slipped away as Sir Edward helped me onto the beach. There I stood, water streaming off me in all directions. How light it was already, the sky the color of goldenrods, the sea all gilded swells and shadowed troughs.

"Your lips aren't even blue," said Sir Edward. "Here, wrap this around you, anyway."

I draped the jacket over my head like a hood, and around my shoulders and chest. Wet hair, plastered to my scalp, might look very unlike a wig. And the growing Corinna, in a wet tunic, even less like a Folk Keeper. It was Sir Andrew's jacket; Sir Edward had not wanted to give up his own.

"Lady Alicia won't like it that you let Finian fall off the cliff," I said.

"She won't," said Sir Edward. "I shall have to admit to her that we quarreled, and that when he shoved me I was childish enough to shove him back, and so it went."

"You quarreled about his costume?"

He shrugged. "It all seems so unimportant now."

"What if he dies?"

"You're a cool little thing, aren't you. *What if he dies*, you ask, calm as can be." He pointed down the beach to a broad backside bent over a long body. "The problem was not that Finian can't swim, but that he hit his head. Mrs. Bains is doing what she can."

I did not feel like a cool little thing. There was a terrible emptiness in my stomach, and I kept thinking of all the things I'd never said to Finian. Did he know I treasured the amber beads? Did he know I even laughed at his jokes, deep inside? I could not imagine how it must be for Lady Alicia, who leaned against the cliff. A scrap of gold satin lay on the crumbled rock, a piece of morning sky come to earth. She is very brave. I will never know what a mother feels when she waits to learn if her son lives or dies.

I was suddenly seized in a plush embrace. "Bless the boy!" cried Mrs. Bains. She was still wearing her housekeeper slippers. "He asked for you, Master Finian did. Asked for you then laughed a bit—you know the way he has—and said, 'Tell Samson not to cut his hair!'"

Finian would live! Oh, the relief of it—my stomach filled up and my mind emptied out. I could wonder for the first time how Mrs. Bains had managed the cliff path; I could almost laugh at the thought that she'd need a winch to help her up again.

The Valet and his scornful cousins appeared, rather out of breath, with eiderdown quilts and a bottle of amber liquid. I glanced Finian's way, then wished I hadn't. His wet hair was dark and dead-looking on the rock. I'd rather remember him from last night, when the firelight shone through his hair, shooting it with red lights.

The footmen exchanged looks of dismay when Mrs. Bains said it was time to carry Finian up the cliff.

"Up with you, too, Master Corin!" Mrs. Bains's heavy hand was on my shoulder. "Come get warm, Saints love you."

My feet were sure and light up the cliff path. It was as though I had just then memorized the cliff, learned by heart its craggy tapestry. Where did clumsy Corinna go?

I look into the bedchamber mirror, which now reflects the twilight sky. Is this the old clumsy me, or the new surefooted one?

I must tend the Folk. I missed my chance to gather Saint-John's-Wort at Midsummer dawn. How shall I control the Folk during the Feast of the Keeper?

My Folk Bag leans against the dressing table, looking rather full. Of course, it is the peat. I told Sir Andrew I will never marry, and that is the truth. But I may as well break it open, just to amuse myself.

I am back, staring into the twilight mirror. It is all silliness, and wouldn't Finian laugh if he knew that the strands that bind my peat are dark red.

10

Including *Balymas Day* (the *Feast of the Keeper* Is Tomorrow!)

June 23

Clumsy Corinna is back. How can it be that my body did what I asked of it for only one night? I miss the skipping freedom of that Midsummer girl. Who can explain it: How did she come? Where did she go? I've been looking for her.

I dropped off the edge of the beach today, into water to my waist. After a few rocky steps, I slipped and came up spluttering. Where was that new dimension, the sudden electrical opening of the world?

Finian has been weak and ill. Mrs. Bains delights in trapping him under trays of broths and gruels and iced jellies. She wanted me to take to bed, too. "All that time in the nasty sea, and you such a little thing!"

"I am never chilled," I tell her, and close my ears against her entreaties. Closing my ears—I revel in it. It is a new power.

If anything, I am rather too warm. I am always flushed these days of summer, my skin surging to rose in the midday sun. No, it is heat, not cold, that affects me most.

The Folk are unnaturally quiet, resting up, perhaps, for the Feast of the Keeper, now fewer than two weeks away. I have no charms now; I missed my chance to gather Saint-John's-Wort.

The easy days are gone.

July 4—Balymas Day

I almost welcome Taffy's companionship. He's curled beside me on the cliff top, but I do not go so far as to pat him when he asks. His fur is sticky and old, worn down to the skin. He does not insist, however, and I tell him that at least his manners are good. His tail thuds on the rock.

The Folk continue quiet. They have consumed:

> One barrel of herring
> One dozen lobsters, with most of the
> shell.

Mrs. Bains was not pleased. She was hoping to have one of those lobsters for herself. Today Finian has consumed:

> A dram of ginger wine
> Bread with milk and honey
> A bowl of egg pudding.

He is pale and spends much of the day in his room, but I've coaxed him to come sailing with me tomorrow.

The Feast of the Keeper is the day after that, and then I shall be obliged to return to the old way of spending hour upon hour in the Cellar.

I will not allow Taffy to join me. He is old and fragile, and any sputter of anger from the Folk might kill him. I shall be alone again, just me and the Folk.

And another worry, too. I am growing. What will Mrs. Bains think when I tell her I need new and different clothes, tight waistcoats and loose frock coats? Sometimes I grow weary of it all, the pretense, the worry about the Folk. Finian once asked what would be so bad about becoming a gentleman. What if I revealed everything and became—what? A lady, I suppose. Do ladies sail? Would they take away my amber beads?

No, if I cannot be a Sir Edward, running the estate and doing as I like, I'd best remain a Folk Keeper.

July 5

Only one day later, and the world is running in reverse, right to left, against the tide of expectation. I am in the Cellar where I belong, in the cold and the damp and the dark.

How different from the clear Cliffsend light earlier today. Even the rocks were shining when I scrambled down the cliff, too intent on reaching the pier to see what I should have seen from above. *The Lady Rona* was gone, already out to sea, heading for the Seal Rock. Periwinkle water stretched between boat and shore; the *Windcuffer* and I were left behind.

The round, whole world as I'd known it cracked in my hands and leaked through my fingers. "Come back!"

But it was too late. Finian was soon nothing more than a sail against the round bowl of the horizon.

I wanted to pluck the plug from that basin and watch him drain into the center of the world. And with that fancy came a mounting pressure inside, like an egg left cooking too long. Off I'd go, *Pop!* Bits of shell striking everyone.

I seized a stone and ran to the end of the pier. *Smash!* In it would go, into the *Windcuffer*, through those mahogany floorboards Finian loved so well.

I raised it over my head. The stone trembled in my grasp, but my fingers wouldn't release it. I had grown soft all these weeks away from my Cellar.

Very gently, I laid it on the pier, sat down beside it. I spoke aloud to the sea, my words skipping like smooth stones over an underwater storm. "I propose a pact. Grow angry, as I am. Toss Finian around a bit. I haven't the strength to frighten him, but you have."

It was a childish game, urging the sea to take my revenge for me. "In return, I vow to worship you all the days of my life."

Someone was coming up behind; I pressed my lips together.

"Why didn't Finian take the *Windcuffer*?" It was Sir Edward. "He always sails the *Windcuffer*."

"Not always, it would seem." I had also wondered why, but what was it to him? "Might I borrow a knife?" I said. Then, at his look of surprise, "Or your brooch? Yes, the cameo. I'll only be a moment."

It was just like Sir Edward to have a good, sharp clasp to his brooch. I jabbed the pin into my fingertip, where it leaked blood, but nothing of my rage. One, two, three, I shook the red drops into the sea and whispered, "To our pact, strong as blood!"

"Whatever are you doing?" said Sir Edward. But before I could tell him it was none of his affair, his voice changed and he pointed to the sea. "Look!" His hand still bore the livid crescent of my teeth from Midsummer.

Quick as mercury, the sea's periwinkle face turned dark and rough. The waves arched with anger, like a cat, running with the wind at their backs. Against the darkening horizon, the air grew yellow; the solitary boat rocked in long combers.

The pier was not large enough for my feelings. It was a child's game, my pact with the sea. Surely it hadn't raised a storm? I brushed past Sir Edward. "Did he have an amber bead?" I said aloud. I had not one, but two. I paced the beach, watching the waves swell, the foam gather along their backs and streak in the direction of the wind.

I had to walk, I had to move, but Sir Edward stood curiously still, just watching. Monarch butterflies lay motionless at my feet. Against the shore, waves threw chunks of rock from their yawning bellies.

The coming storm was a tangle of sounds: Taffy whining from the cliffs, the wind keening across the waves, the sudden silence of birds. The air turned to pea soup; I could no longer see the white speck of Finian's boat.

"It was just a game," I cried to the sea. "I take it back!" But the rain came anyway, great hard drops that stung my face and pounded fragile butterfly wings.

Throughout it all, Sir Edward stood motionless on

the pier, just watching, black satin drenched by cold rain. He said not a word of warning or encouragement as I pushed past him for the second time and almost fell into the *Windcuffer*, cursing the random, erratic winds. The *Windcuffer* shot away from the pier, rearing back to leap the waves, pitching so hard into troughs it seemed she must tear a hole in the fabric of the sea.

The waves snatched the amber bead from my palm. "For smooth sailing!" I screamed, but the sea had forgotten the rules, or else it was too late. My fingertip wept blood. Salt wind stung my eyes, a lone gull flew past.

I made for the Seal Rock in the mysterious way a pigeon heads for home. But I wasn't even halfway there before the giant palm of one of those waves slapped at the *Windcuffer*. I slammed into the mast, and precious seconds passed before I could breathe again, before I realized that the water lapping about my ankles hadn't come from the sea and crashing waves.

I pressed my hand to the floor. My finger fit comfortably into a crack between the boards. How did the flooring come to be damaged? The sea below was filling up the *Windcuffer* faster than the sky from above.

The flooring gave way. The waves were on it in a second, biting and tearing at it, pulling it apart with frothy fingers.

I watched the sea gradually merging with the *Windcuffer*, and the *Windcuffer* gradually merging with the sea. The boat I'd helped bring to life fell to bits about me, and then I hardly cared that I also merged with the water, now pounded beneath as a wave crested, now tossed to the surface by some boiling power beneath.

Pictures flitted through my head like dreams. White water swallowing a bit of planking, dense silver needles of rain. A hand lying against silvered fur. My hand, and my arms, too, wrapped about a round neck, my chest pressed close to a sleek back. These were no common seals ringed round me, with their great silver heads and deep human eyes.

I closed my own eyes. "May our boat be blessed."

Smashing water is nothing to the Sealfolk. We ran effortlessly with the waves, riding them easily as foam. *Boom* and *Hiss*, went the waves. *Boom* and *Hiss*. I was all but one with the sea. And Finian, how he would love this. Where was he?

Boom and *Hiss*.

Was he alive?

As we entered the cove, the song of the waves turned into a steady crashing, and there were human voices, too, calling my name. The storm had lost heart, content just to spit the waves about. I could stand alone; the water came to my chest.

Behind me, the Sealfolk were already racing out to sea. "Come back!" But it was too late.

"Corin!"

My head snapped forward. It was Finian—Finian!—hurrying over the scatter of low-tide rocks, now plunging through the water toward me.

"You idiot!" he cried. "Taking the *Windcuffer* into that storm!"

"You're alive!" I did not shout as he had, but he heard me nonetheless.

"Imagine that!" he said. "Unlike you, I came back the

moment the storm began. And now the *Windcuffer's* gone."

"The Sealfolk brought me back." I could not stop thinking of it.

"I must have called them," said Finian. "*Seven tears to call the Sealfolk.* I wept enough tears to call dozens."

"You can't call the Sealfolk at low tide."

Then Sir Edward stood beside us, and I had to gulp back the words that were clamoring to leap from my mouth. *Why did you leave me behind?*

"You must hurry, Corin," said Sir Edward. "One of the calves has taken ill, and some of the cheeses have melted into pools of whey. The Folk are angry, and I fear for my crops."

"Give Corin a chance to draw his breath!" said Finian.

But for once, I agreed with Sir Edward. The Folk Keeper must hurry when the Folk grow wild. So I said only to Finian, "I'm sorry about the *Windcuffer.*"

I don't remember scaling the cliff. Sir Edward might have helped me, clumsy again as I am. I do remember the endless pounding of my feet across the grass, thinking strange disjointed thoughts. How could the Folk have grown wild when the Feast of the Keeper wasn't until to-morrow? How could the grass be dry when everything else had been so wet? Then I was pounding up marble steps and down marble corridors to seize my Folk Bag. I had no time to examine it, but I am careful and I knew it held everything it should: my necklet of nails and my writing lead, and then—all wrapped in oilcloth against the Cellar's damp—this Folk Record and my tinderbox and candles. I had no time to gather bread or salt or churchyard mold. But I could not go without an offering of food. Quick: to the Kitchens.

The Cellar was very quiet. I laid down my offering and edged open the Folk Door. It felt quiet enough, but perhaps the Folk had spent all their wild energy on the calf and the cheeses.

For perhaps the first time, I do not want to be here. I find myself trapped; I see no way out. I'm afraid I may fail with the Folk. I'm afraid the Folk may injure me. But I am also afraid to reveal my secret, ask to become a lady, as Lord Merton had originally intended. Even if Sir Edward didn't turn me away, I might spend my life waiting on one pier or another. I refuse to wait, and worry, and indulge myself in all the peculiar feelings most people are so fond of. I refuse!

Why did Finian leave me waiting?

Two hours have passed while I've been writing. There is still no sign of the Folk. Could Sir Edward be wrong?

But while a calf might sicken of itself, it can be no natural thing that the cheeses melted into whey.

For now, however, the Folk are quiet, and I am back in the dark where I belong.

11

The *Feast of the Keeper*, but What Is It to Me?

July 6—Feast of the Keeper

I said I belong in the dark and the deep, and now my words are coming back, mocking me. But how could I have known? My own deep darkness—it has nothing to do with the Cellar. Yet look where I am, on this, the Feast of the Keeper!

Ah, Corinna, stop. Just be thankful you have your Folk Bag, and that your Folk Record is still dry because it was properly wrapped in oilcloth, and that you have enough light to write in it, too. At least you can talk to yourself.

It was an entire lifetime ago when I sat in the Cellar yesterday, a whole world ago when the Cellar door opened and there came soft footsteps, and a light. I did not even look up when the footsteps stood before me; I could see well enough who it was by the white silk stockings and black rosettes on his shoes.

"Finian has taken ill again," said Sir Edward. "Very ill. We're all gathered in the churchyard to pray."

I rose without a word.

"Quietly now through the Manor," said Sir Edward. "We must do nothing to disturb Finian."

The night was warmer than I'd expected, the graveyard dark and still. "The others are all so quiet," I whispered.

"They are praying."

I paused at the gate. "They are not even breathing."

"Trust you to notice, you with that hearing of yours."

I should have heeded the little prickle that came to the back of my neck, but would it have done any good? Sir Edward was walking me to the tiny grave under the chapel eaves, and his grip was very tight at my elbow.

"There is no one here." I paused, smelling recently turned earth, rotting wood, and mildew. "You disturbed the baby's grave!"

A taste like spoiled apples rose in my throat, and the details of that scene froze themselves in memory. Me, looking down, seeing an ivy-covered mound, my worn boots, Sir Edward's black rosettes. It was a quarter past one.

"No one but you will notice," he said. "No one comes here much, and I've covered the raw earth with leaves and ivy."

Something was terribly wrong, but perhaps something was also terribly right. "Finian is not really ill, is he?"

"He's well enough to be looking for you in Firth Landing, making sure you haven't stolen aboard the Mainland ferry. I told him you'd crept away from the Cellar. He didn't even stop to look for you there, just went searching. And as you were to be found nowhere on the estate, what would he conclude but that you'd run away?"

"I didn't run away!"

Sir Edward shrugged. "Finian seemed to think he might even be responsible. Half the serving staff is scattered about Cliffsend, looking for you. The Manor won't be this empty again until the Harvest Fair, when everyone down to the scullery maid takes a three-day holiday."

"Liar! I never left the Cellar."

"I must make you understand." He pressed at my shoulder, I sank to my knees. His candle shone on the tiny gravestone.

> *Unnamed from the darkness came.*
> *Unnamed to the darkness returned.*
> *Born and died: Midsummer Eve.*

I saw what I'd not before realized. "My birthday!"

A terrible darkness poured itself into my mind; my muscles gathered of themselves to leap away, but Sir Edward snatched me from the air as though I were a sparrow and tossed me onto the grave.

"Damn!" He pressed his finger to my collar-bone, pinning me in place. "My candle has gone out. No screaming, or I shall have to stop you, like this."

He squeezed my throat, trapping the old air inside. I struggled beneath his hand. Everyone thinks breathing in is so important; no one thinks about breathing out.

Sir Edward relaxed his grip. "You'll not try again, will you?"

I shook my head, whispered, "What do you want?"

"I want to know what Finian knows. He sees too much, that boy; he's made more trouble for me than I care to admit."

"What Finian knows?" I repeated stupidly.

"Does he know who your mother is?"

"My mother?"

"Ah!" said Sir Edward, and laughed. He turned my head on its pillow of dirt. Directly ahead lay the Lady Rona's weathered headstone.

Another frozen moment: a dimpled moon, an ivory cheek, the smell of fresh-turned rot. Twenty-seven minutes past one.

My mother. I might have denied it, but etched into my memory was the inscription on the gravestone. *Midsummer Eve.* A holiday never celebrated on the Mainland, one I'd never connected with my birthday.

"But the baby died at birth," I whispered at last.

"So you didn't know!" said Sir Edward, and his fingers relaxed on my throat. "Then perhaps Finian hasn't worked out the real story for himself. I only have just today. Hartley tricked me into believing the baby died, just as he always tricked me. Tell me this: Did Finian know about the Lady Rona, know she was a Sealmaiden? Which means, of course, that you are, too."

Bolts of lightning might have struck my temples. I was dizzy, my thoughts buzzing uselessly, beads on a vibrating string. "I'm no Sealmaiden!" The mere sound of it is soft and tender. Not like me.

"It's the old story," said Sir Edward. "Your father out

for a moonlight sail. Your mother dancing on the Seal Rock. He fell in love with her, stole her Sealskin, insisted she marry him, live on land. What could she do? Without her Sealskin she couldn't return to the sea. Perhaps you can guess at the rest. Misery, jealousy, madness, and death."

"What makes you think I'm her daughter?"

"You gave yourself away by calling up that storm."

"Calling up the storm?" But already I realized what I had done. The sea cared nothing for my pact. It cared only for my blood. *Three drops of Sealfolk blood to call up a storm.*

To think that I had almost killed Finian! Really, I might have, with my casual vengeance. *Finian.* I wanted to say his name again and again, place him firmly on the earth, where he was usually solid enough. *Finian!* said my mind, but I forced myself to attend to Sir Edward.

"I'm a careful man," he said. "I knew you must be of the Sealfolk, but I couldn't be sure you were Rona's daughter until I opened the grave. There are no little bones in that coffin. The story of your death was just that, a story Hartley gave out."

"I refuse to be his daughter!" Not that hateful man with the dead metal eyes.

"You refuse him just as he refused you. He was entranced by your mother, but you were not an attractive baby, and he must have come a little to his senses. A Merton can't have one of the Sealfolk as his heir. It would be so like him to give out that you'd died, but instead have you sent away where he could keep track of you from afar."

"Knowing about me, his baby, all those years?" I hated Lord Merton more than ever. "Having the Matrons inform him when I was moved from Home to Home?" I'd fooled him once, though. He hadn't known I'd become Corin. He'd known Corinna was sent to the Rhysbridge Home, but no one had known to tell him she'd turned into a boy.

"How he loved to control people," said Sir Edward. "I could never escape it. Now he'd dangle the Manor in front of my nose. *You shall inherit it,* he'd say. Now he'd say he rather thought he'd get married again. *My bride shall take the estate, and her son after her.* Perhaps he fetched you back to Cliffsend because he could not bear to lose control of you, even when he was dead."

"But he couldn't bear to let me inherit, either?"

Sir Edward shook his head. "Although as between you and Finian, there's little to choose."

Oh, I understood him then. The estate was Sir Edward's blood, his life, but as Lord Merton's daughter, I stood in his way. So did Lady Alicia and Finian.

"I mean to marry Alicia," said Sir Edward. "She will have me, I am almost sure, if that son of hers doesn't stick his nose where it's not wanted. And then I shall be master of Marblehaugh Park by marriage, not by blood. Wouldn't Hartley be surprised!"

He seized the front of my shirt and pulled me to my feet. What a long walk that was, Sir Edward's fingers wrapped round the back of my neck, steering me past the vacant eyes of the chapel Saints to the wall circling the shaft into the Caverns.

"You mean to put me in there!"

"We shall get through the Feast of the Keeper very well," said Sir Edward. "I have every expectation of a good harvest with the Folk quiet and content from their sacrifice."

"Me, as sacrifice!" But I couldn't be afraid of that, when first I had to be afraid of dying as I fell into the Caverns. "You won't have a live sacrifice."

"Listen: There's a stream beneath." Sir Edward held up his finger. From deep underground came the sound of running water magnified by a cavernous space. "Others have survived the fall through the Graveyard Shaft, so will you." He turned me by the shoulders so my back was pressed into the stone, my face full in the moonlight.

"But the Folk won't touch me. I have the power of The Last Word."

Sir Edward shook his head. "It all comes together for me, now that I know you're no boy. How did you manage so well all these months as Folk Keeper without that power?"

He shook his head. "You are so very like your mother. Those broad cheekbones, those eyes, set slightly at a slant. I can't imagine how I didn't see it. But Rona's baby was a girl, and it never occurred to me you could be a boy. Your disguise as Folk Keeper was a good one."

"Did I have a Sealskin?" I bit down on my lip, but too late, the question was out. Corinna, never never again let your enemy know what might be precious to you!

"Now there's a question," said Sir Edward. "If you had, Hartley might have destroyed it. He burned your mother's; that's when she went mad, refused ever again to look at the sea."

I knew then the taste of true fear. It tastes of dark places deep in your stomach and holds you by the neck, tighter than Sir Edward ever could. I must have tried to leap away, for my next memory is of Sir Edward holding me by the wrist, my Folk Bag lying at my feet.

"I've hunted long enough that I can tell when an animal's about to bolt. Don't try again or I shall become annoyed."

I was choking with fear and the unspent energy of that leap. I bared my teeth and lunged. I missed his neck, found his shoulder.

"Vixen!" Hard knuckles struck my head, which affected me somehow in my middle, for the next thing I remember is being very sick all over a pair of satin rosettes.

Very carefully, I settled the Folk Bag over my shoulder. "Are you annoyed now?" And I bit him in the arm.

The rest is just a confused struggle, me trying to bite him, him bolting my arms tightly to my sides—which at least kept me attached to my Bag—scraping my back up the Shaft. My last frozen memory is looking into his forget-me-not eyes, seeing the livid scar behind his eyebrow, then falling, falling, clinging to my Bag, breaking through water, sinking deep, hitting rock, shooting up again.

It was fresh water.

"Corin! Corinna!" Sir Edward's voice sounded faintly through the Graveyard Shaft. "Corinna, answer me!"

I swam about blindly. I could not tell where the stream ended, or if the stream ended. There was only the echo of Sir Edward's voice to tell me which way was up. It seems odd now as I write this, but there, flailing about in the water, I was mostly full of a joyful rage. I wouldn't give Sir Edward the satisfaction of my being eaten by the Folk. My Folk Bag was properly packed, candles and tinderbox wrapped in oilcloth. The Folk would not come near a lighted candle.

I splashed about, slapping water, slapping more water, finally slapping stone. I eased myself onto the bank.

"Corinna! Corin!"

I shook myself at the edge of the stream. "Corin! Corinna!" I said nothing, and shedding water makes no sound.

"Corin! Corinna!" Let him think I'd perished!

He called until dawn bloomed in the patch of sky through the Shaft. His final shout of "Corin!" turned into a cry of horror as a stream of smoke poured itself downward, past his head.

The bats had returned home on this, the morning of the Feast of the Keeper. The Folk won't eat me, Sir Edward, and I know why. May your crops fail, Sir Edward; may your milk spoil.

And when you ask for her hand in marriage, may Lady Alicia slap your face.

July 11

My hair reaches past my shoulders. Two inches a day it grows. Even if I didn't have my internal clock, I'd know I've been here six days. I've tried spreading my clothes on the floor, but they are always a bit damp, dreadful to put on. This morning I turned out my pockets and found a single amber bead. I hurled it from me. It bounced off the floor and rolled into a corner.

I need no protection against the sea. And I need little against the Folk. They can't attack me here, as long as a glimmer of starlight seeps through the Graveyard Shaft. I need no salt or churchyard mold. I need only light. I must save my candles for the first overcast night. Sir Edward may know about hunting, but he knows nothing about the Folk. I do. I am partly of the Other-folk and have always had an instinct for the world of spells and magic.

I am not quite alone.

A cave rat lives in a pile of shredded bark, and of course, there are the bats. To say that the Cavern is filled with bats is like saying the ocean is filled with drops. The Cavern *is* bats. They fill the walls like water lilies, fantastic flower-heads between folded leaf-wings. Once I tried to count a small patch of them. It was impossible.

And so this is my Cavern; it is really very beautiful. The roof is like water turned to stone, tumbled falls, shining always faintly from the wet. Mushrooms sprout from invisible crevices. But they do not even tempt me, because of course, there are the fish.

The fish, so innocent, so trusting. They are not accustomed to the creature with the five white fingers that dangle languorously into the water. They swim into my grasp; I eat and eat and eat. There is a kind of savage joy in not thinking of feeding the Folk. I never set food aside for them now. Let the stupid, sulky things take care of themselves!

I am lucky, though, that I can catch my own supper. If I were an ordinary human, hunger might drive me to light one of my precious candles and wander through that dark archway at the far end of this chamber, looking for the path to the outside, and to food. But I am the lucky one. I have the luxury of eating and even of tossing aside what I do not care to eat. When it thinks I am not looking, the rat carries away the entrails and skeletons.

I don't waste much breath calling up the Shaft. Even if there were anyone near, I doubt my voice would carry above the ground.

To pass the time, I have been reading through this Folk Record. How crisp and fresh it seemed in February, when I'd just started a new one. But it is no longer a Folk Record: I relinquish my duties! Call it instead Corinna's Journal.

Again and again I have said I belong to the cold and the dark and the wet. I was right and I was wrong. I belong to the dark and the wet of the sea. I was once a girl who became a boy who became a Folk Keeper. Now I am a girl again, looking for a way to become a Seal-maiden.

I must find a way out.

July 12

Another day gone, another two inches to my hair. I wear it now in a braid. I have read more of my Journal and I realize something that makes my heart squeeze in on itself—a good reason not to have a heart! I have been reading backward through the pages, thus:

> *July 6, from Corinna:*
> *Did I have a Sealskin?*

June 22, from Finian:
> *You've grown a bit since, but no matter. I*
> *can surely help you over the flames.*

March 22, from Sir Edward:
> *I wish they'd destroyed the silvery skin*
> *instead. It looks to be ruined in any event,*
> *as it is somehow stretching.*

March 21, from Sir Edward:
> *Hartley took a number of silvery ones over*
> *the years, mostly smaller, as I recall.*

March 21, from Lady Alicia:
> *Isn't he a bit bigger? I'd swear he's grown*
> *since he first came.*

My senses are peeling away from me. My fingertips are far away in the Trophy Room, running themselves over a silver skin, but they are also here, writing.

His Lordship's prize trophy: It is my Sealskin! There were not a number of *silvery ones* as Sir Edward thought. There was only one, but it has been growing as I have been growing.

Everything shivers into place. This explains my strange yearnings, my thirst for something unknowable, my unusual abilities and limitations.

The important thing is this: I am missing a piece. A piece as real as an arm or an eye. I always knew something was missing, that I was a shadow at noon, melting away beneath my own two feet. Once I feel my Sealskin round me, once I press it to my skin, I shall be whole.

His Lordship's prize trophy—it is me, and I have been growing as my Sealskin has been growing.

I am filled with a boundless rage when I think of Lord Merton watching me from the Trophy Room, watching his prize trophy grow. I spit on his memory, set the hounds on his soul. He destroyed my mother, but he shan't destroy me.

No, it is not hunger—stomach hunger—that will drive me through the dark opening at the far end of this chamber. I may be a long time finding my way, but they are all connected, these Caverns, and one path or another will lead me to the Folk Door.

I am no Folk Keeper. I am a Sealmaiden, and I know where I belong.

Tomorrow then, when my braid has grown another two inches, I will light the first of my candles and walk into that dark tunnel, remembering always that on the other end waits my Sealskin.

12

Including the *Feast of Dolores, the Skeptic* (and Other Feast Days I Do Not Care to Name)

July 13

The Folk were everywhere present, there in the twisted passageways and echoing Caverns where the sun never shines. Their boiling energy retreated from my candle as I entered the first tunnel. Have they lingered there and sniffed at me, licking their lips?

The walls were heavy draperies, stone folded upon stone, lustrous with damp. I counted my steps for comfort, walking slowly. Horrible thought, to fall and lose my candle. The passage forked at three hundred paces. I shone my candle down each branch. The left-hand branch narrowed and dipped sharply. But the branch to my right was easy and spacious, and as far as my light would reach, rose steadily toward the surface.

I wore my necklet of nails, from habit only. It had

never shielded me from these Folk. But I had another use for it now. I scratched a *C* into the soft walls, marking my turn to the right.

The passage did not live up to its early promise. It rose only a bit, then leveled off, and more and more the walls ran with wet. For almost five hundred paces, the tunnel walls pressed close around me, and when they fell away at last, invisible antennae on my backbone rose to meet a vast space.

The walls here were a marvel, delicate filaments of stone swirling over and in on themselves. I held up the candle; it strained into an enormous darkness. A forest of stone icicles winked down at me, my flame caught at thousands of sharp, wet points. A cold drop landed on my cheek, then on my forehead as I leaned back. A stone straw, dripping water from above. I opened my mouth and snatched a drop from the air.

I explored this new chamber cautiously, hugging the walls, wondering if they circled in on themselves or opened into other tunnels. I wore no shoes, and before I saw what lay ahead, my feet splashed into shallow water. A cave pool, edged with rocky lace. A clutch of stone pearls shone from the bottom, flat stone pancakes floated on the top. Then, in this place where even the water was gray, something beyond the pool gleamed yellow-white.

Bones. Fine hand bones, human icicles. I was not afraid; I was barely surprised, in the vast, calm silence of the Caverns. My eyes traveled along more icicle-bones to the head, which smiled mournfully at me.

I cannot say what possessed me to draw near. Perhaps I knew I'd see the square marks of those teeth that had also marked my offerings of meat in the Cellar.

The Folk had been at work here, long ago perhaps. I leaned over the skeleton and held my candle into the darkness beyond. My candle shook—no, it was I who shook. I held it with two hands, and then it shook all the more!

The Folk indeed had been at work, but not so very long ago. Scraps of fabric lay scattered about. The Folk had had to undress their meal, and they'd not been tidy about it. I knew those crimson stripes, the livery of Marblehaugh Park. I knew with dreadful certainty that the livery belonged to Old Francis. So did the bones.

Others have survived the fall, Sir Edward had said. I was not his first live sacrifice for the Folk, human sacrifice. He'd used the Shaft rather than the Folk Door, which is never locked. This is why I survived the Storms of the Equinox. The Folk were already brimful of holiday cheer—and Old Francis.

I waited until my hands were steady before resuming my trip round the chamber. I could not leave this casual graveyard; I did not have that luxury. What if a passage to the Folk Door led from here?

There were none, however; the chamber was self-enclosed. I hardly cared. It was such a relief to come full circle to the chamber entrance, down the tunnel to the *C* I'd scratched in stone, sweet evidence Corinna really existed. From there, it was just moments to the friendly twilight of my own chamber, hung with bats, forested with mushrooms, flowing with fish too guileless to evade the snatching skeleton of my own hand.

July 14
Five minutes to ten o'clock, morning. I stumbled over

117

another skeleton, literally. It was only a goat, I think, but still I apologized.

July 15

Half past midnight. Why did Finian leave me on the pier?

July 16

Thirty-one minutes past two o'clock, afternoon. I snatched a ghost-fish from an underground stream. Its skin was absolutely transparent, all its inner workings on display. For eyes, just sightless pearls, sealed by filmy skin. No need for sight where the sun never shines.

All the tunnels end in disappointment.

I have used two candles.

July 19

Forty-six minutes past nine o'clock, evening. I wonder if the Folk made great mischief on the Feast of the Keeper? I scratch the letter *C* into every turn to mark my trail, but all tunnels end in disappointment. I think of my mother, scratching her name into the Cellar walls. When her Sealskin was destroyed, she turned away from the sea. It must have been too painful to set eyes on it again. But neither could she quite let go of her need for a deep, dark place. The Cellar was perhaps the closest she could come.

I have used four candles.

July 20

Six o'clock, morning. Why did Finian leave me on

the pier? He said that he wept. Was it for the *Windcuffer*?

July 22

Noon, exactly. I wonder why my father had me brought to Cliffsend? Sir Edward thought he could not bear to lose control of me, but perhaps it's not that simple. Perhaps he regretted what he'd done. Could he not have been speaking of himself when he said: *He told me of your existence, of his shame that he placed you in a foundling home?* I will never know.

All tunnels end in disappointment.

I have used seven candles.

July 27

Half past five o'clock, morning. I have one candle left.

Feast of Dolores, the Skeptic—I will not mark the date

I cannot break the habit of writing. I do not want to write, I am too low in spirit, but my hand moves on. I do not care to count the days, but there are other ways of marking time. My hair has grown past my waist. My braid, I should say, its weave relaxing more each day. Last night was perfectly dark, no moonlight, or starlight even, penetrated the Graveyard Shaft. I do not count the days, yet my hand knows this is the Feast of Dolores, the Skeptic. It leaps to the paper to write of the Folk.

I went to sleep, sick with worry that I had only one candle. But on this moonless, starless night, I should have gone to sleep worried about the unalloyed dark. I found myself sitting up, awakened by a change in the pressure of the air about me. They were upon me, they were all over me—oh, they must be ravenous.

I shook my puny necklet at them, but it hadn't stopped them before and it didn't now. They boiled in on me. Theirs is a touch almost without weight, and yet worse, for it sinks beneath the skin, running needles of fire through sinew and bone. My arm was already turning numb when a fresh, hot pain skewered my hip.

Oh, for the power of The Last Word. What would rhyme? What would scan? But even asking the question defeats the meaning, for The Last Word must be a rhyme so original, springing so spontaneously to the mind, there's no room for thought.

Now their touch had weight. Something hard sank into my arm, something wet lapped my hand.

"Saints save me!"

The Folk moaned back at the invocation of the Saints. I leapt for the tinderbox. Just one spark, and there came a terrible shrieking that would have shattered my bones—if I'd had any left to shatter.

It took three tries for my accursed clumsy fingers to light the candle, but at each new spark, the shrieking sounded farther, and by the time the candle finally caught, I was alone.

I was alone, my flame quivering from the quivering in my hand, my arm a mass of blood.

I sat all night holding the candle, never heeding the hot wax falling on my skin. My face was warm, I held it so close. It was not yet dawn when the wick staggered into a pool of wax and was drowned.

July 31—Anniversary of the Liberation of Rhysbridge

The Folk have consumed:

Not quite a bite of Corinna.

The candlewick is little more than dusty air. I squeeze it between my thumb and forefinger and stare at the ashes marking my fingertips. I blow it into my Twilight Cavern.

August 1

Curses on the Folk, curses on Sir Edward. I will circle them with a noose of curses and pull it tight.

Curses on the Folk!

Curses on Sir Edward!

I refuse to be trapped inside my fear of the next moonless, starless night.

I refuse to be trapped inside myself! Why am I still pretending to be a boy, hanging onto the habit of wearing these damp clothes, of binding back my hair? If I die under a siege of strong, square teeth, I refuse to die as Corin the Folk Keeper. I will die as Corinna the Seal-maiden.

August 2

The world is an explosion of beauty. My senses have opened like flowers; everything is an exquisite pleasure. I taste . . .

What I taste just kneeling beside the stream! I taste the spicy smell of leaves that wash in from the outside. It resonates in a sensitive spot beneath my tongue. The rat brings damp wood into the cave. It tastes light and dark together, deep in the corner of my jaw.

I feel.

Each fingertip is a separate small heartbeat that acknowledges the other small lives all around. The smooth, damp pull of the skin of a mushroom. It is full of life. I scoop a spider from the floor. Its weightless legs leave tiny vibrations on my palm. I bring my finger to my cheek. They greet each other. Two consciousnesses, brought together.

I see.

Human eyes, or even the eyes of a Sealmaiden, are little good deep below the earth, but my . . .

Oh, I will not give it away at once. I will delight in the telling of it, in every detail of how it unfolded.

This morning I turned myself inside out, turned Corin into Corinna. Off came Corin's jacket, his loose linen shirt, his breeches. Why did I wear them so long? Here they can stay. What the cave rat doesn't steal for its nest can molder with damp.

How light and free I felt. Had I ever had so much air on my body? I never knew I had so much skin, the bluish-pale skin of the Sealfolk, all underlaced with blue veins.

And when I loosened my braid and raked my fingers through the weave of hair:

The world shifted about me, and did not come again to rest. I'd thought the world was full of bounded space, described by walls and footmen and cliffs and coal scuttles. That's only the smallest part of it. The air is always shifting, boiling around you, full of mysterious and wonderful things to see—if you only know how to see!

I can see with my hair. When I move, the air bounces off the nearest object, then returns, bearing a description of where it's been. I take a step: I see the curl of stone draperies high in the roof. I push my palm toward the bat-velvet walls: I can count the bats! There are sixteen hanging in a palm-sized space. I catch an air-sculpture of the cave rat scuttling behind me, quivering whiskers, short legs. How often has it done so when my back was turned?

For four years I have been wearing blinders. I thought all this time I walked a path of cobblestones, and it turns out to have been an avenue of stars! For four years, my head has been caught in a box. Its sides were painted with pleasant enough scenes, but that I should have thought this was the world!

I do not need to look back in my Folk Record to remember that the Lady Rona wore her hair long and loose, that she could walk through crowded rooms with her eyes shut. Remember, Corinna—clumsy Corinna!— how astonished you were to hear that! Remember how in darkness she scrawled her name into the Cellar walls?

You are more like your mother than you think.

August 5

I no longer stumble. Now I understand why I could circle the Manor on Midsummer Eve without falling. Why I could leap the fire, run along the cliffs to Finian's rescue. It was no Midsummer magic, it was my hair, grown to masquerade as Samson. It's a joy now to walk about the floor without stubbing my toe. A joy to gauge precisely the height of a step. I have been realigned, made true.

I can now make my way through the chamber in deepest darkness, stirring invisible eddies of motion. They shiver off their surroundings and return, translating what they've seen into quivering bits of air. I know the dimension of the Graveyard Shaft, I know the clutter of objects in the rat's nest. My amber bead is one. Keep it, and welcome, cave rat. I won't need it again.

Why did I not have this power when I was eleven and wore my hair long? I grew clumsy when I cut it, but lost no special way of seeing. Who can explain it?

And writing this now, I am telling myself something new. I can find my way through the Caverns with my hair. I don't need candles. What of when I meet the Folk in the Caverns? I still have my tinderbox; I can call sparks into the air and drive them back. And if I can't—better to be eaten alive than return to the old ways.

When I think about Rhysbridge, it seems I was living in a denser darkness than any in these Caverns. I remember the press of houses, the dirty fog, the smell of city filth, the smoky candles, the bruised lips of a dying man.

To think I wanted to stay on as Folk Keeper, living always in the dark. To think that was the end of my ambition! The sea is dark, too, but there—yes, there!—I'll wear my hair long and loose, living always in my own internal light.

13

Harvest Rose Festival to the *Harvest Fair*

August 6—Harvest Rose Festival

The Folk did not frighten me as much as I frightened myself. I paused at the fork in the first tunnel, enjoying the luxury of not fretting about my candles, lingering over that first *C* I'd scratched to mark my first turn. It was a luxury, too, to have turned from Corin to Corinna, to bathe in soft hair to my knees.

It was then I heard it, a dull hammering that made me catch my breath and clutch my tinderbox. A quick spurt, which slowed as I listened, and as I breathed deep, grew slower still. There is an expression about being startled by your own shadow. But what of being startled by your heart, clanging in the silent fortress of your chest? I doubt if anyone's ever laughed in the Caverns before.

Each day it has taken longer to reach unexplored territory. Rarely have I found tunnels that rise toward the surface. Those that do, run into stony blind ends. Today's tunnel led down, not up. My footsteps stuck close beside me as I pattered downward, always downward, then skittered off into an echoing cavern with a deep pit in the floor. At the far end was an interruption in the air, a bulge where no bulge should be. I swung my hair, wrapping invisible streamers round the bulge, divining its shape and texture.

Four limbs and a head—human and not human, all at once. It was not even as tall as I, but made up for it with its thick body and short, powerful limbs. *The Folk are mostly mouth*, Old Francis had said, and he was right. The mouth gaped into its forehead. It had no eyes, not even sightless pearls like the ghost-fish. Perhaps there was a nose, but as it turned toward me, it seemed all wet mouth and square teeth.

It made no sign that I could tell, but another joined it, then another still; and the flint from my tinderbox was barely in my hand before they'd gathered themselves into a mass of hungry darkness. Their energy boiled through my hair, set it almost aflame; and there I was naked, turned inside out, all the soft parts showing.

Sparks, I needed sparks. I raised my flint to strike, when another sort of light burst upon me, an interior illumination. A picture of a silver-haired lady came to me, and words to describe her, too, which wrapped themselves around the image, wove themselves into a net of rhythm and rhyme.

Why weep you in the Manor, Lady?
The Manor, proud and high.
Why scrawl your name in whitewashed
  walls,
When'er your Lord comes neigh?
Why walk about without a word?
Why choose, at last, to die?

That boiling energy, it drained away to nothing. I could paralyze the Folk just as they could paralyze me. Hurt them, too. How they screamed—big babies! I closed my ears against their cries.

I cannot cease my weeping, Sire,
I'm chilled unto the bone.
I've lost my lass, my tiny babe,
I've lost my ancient home.
The singing sea is far, yet near;
I'm locked in solid stone.

It was lovely to see their confusion, knocking against one another and running about. One hurled itself into the pit, and as though they shared one mind, the rest jumped in, too. I hope it was a long way down. Even before I opened my ears, I could tell by the vibration of loose stone that they were still shrieking.

It was only when I was alone with my own friendly heartbeat that I understood. With my hair long and loose, I can carve words from air and float them on a sea of rhyme.

I can always have The Last Word.

August 9

I am still mapping out the Caverns, carving my *C* into each new fork, returning each night to my Twilight Cavern. Today I found two tunnels that rise toward the surface. I call one Hope, the other Anticipation.

The Folk are afraid of me! I string together fluid ropes of verse and beat them off. I've always had the words, I know that now. I had the words, but I didn't have the medium. Just as water dissolves walnuts into dye, my hair dissolves images into rhythm and stirs it all together with rhyme. When I cut my hair to become a Folk Keeper, I took that all away from myself.

There is a price you pay for power.

August 12

Really, what pigs they are, the Folk. The tunnel I call Anticipation is littered with bones and reeks of decay.

It was difficult going today. The passage spiraled sharply upward, and I scrabbled through swirling petals of rock that drew in on themselves, and on me, too! It's lunacy to return to my Twilight Cavern each night and unwind all my hard-won progress. I don't need light, and I shan't want for food and drink. Freshwater streams run everywhere, and even a pearl-eyed fish may be caught and devoured.

August 18

For five days I lived in the dark.

For five days I kept company with the voice of my heart.

For five days I lived in a tunnel called Anticipation, pushing through growing piles of bones.

At half past four on the morning of the sixth day, Anticipation burst open into a vast chamber. Across it curled a small arched door.

I was a long while crossing the chamber, wading through bones at high tide. But then—oh, how well my fingers remembered the Folk Door, the rough wood of it, banded by crosswise strips of iron. But from this side of the Caverns it swung outward, and a whiff of the human world wafted through. There was the familiar smell of mice and damp whitewash, and an old-cheese smell, too.

"Taffy!"

Never have I had such a welcome. He tried to leap on me, but his hindquarters gave. I sank to the floor with him, stroked his sticky fur.

"Taffy!" I said it again and again. "Taffy!" My throat swelled with something irrepressible. How long had it been since I'd wept? I'd forgotten how you can never hold back water. It is accommodating, yet relentless, changing its shape to follow its true path.

It was a long time before I could speak. Even then I didn't say all I understood. That I now knew why Taffy had attached himself to me. He was an older generation of Hill Hound, more closely allied with the Otherfolk— the Sealfolk, and me.

Everything was old but new. The Folk Door, opening in a new direction. Me, feeling a new wetness on my cheek. Me again, seeing old Taffy in a new way. My hair caught the shallow tide of his breath, the thin pulse that keeps him this side of death.

The familiar strangeness didn't end there. The Cellar door was ajar, which was unusual, as everybody was afraid of the Cellar. But why then did no light shine from the landing? The candle was always lit. And where was the smell of baking bread? Cook always baked at dawn.

The Manor was empty. I realized that at once, but I stood at the bottom of the Cellar stairs for many minutes before puzzling out the why of it. Today was August 18, the first day of the Harvest Fair, when all the world was away to celebrate. A day when a Sealmaiden might roam the corridors wearing only her hair and nothing else.

The door between the landing and the Kitchens had been left open, too, and through the long windows onto the vegetable gardens I caught my first glimpse of the out-of-doors. Six weeks of candlelight and darkness, and what did I now see? Wild rains lashing the Manor, bridges of lightning spanning sea and sky.

I broke the silence then. "There is only one other living thing in the Manor, and that is my Sealskin."

I ran now, far faster than old Taffy, pounding down marble corridors, dark rooms flickering past. Into the Trophy Room, past the dead glass eyes. My sleek, shiny Sealskin shimmered out to my hair before I touched it in the ordinary way. It was heavy, tensile, just as a living thing must be.

I wrapped it around me first, paused, wondering if it would take me over at once, turn me into one of the Seal-folk, there on the figured carpet. But nothing happened; it must take salt water to stir human flesh and Sealskin into one.

The Sealskin fit me exactly, falling just to my finger-tips, just to my toes. How marvelous that when I pulled it round my face, each side followed the curve of jaw to meet exactly at my chin. There was nothing wasted, not a single gap. But I had to be closer still. I sank to the floor, pressed it to every part of me. To my naked spine, to my belly and breast, how alive I was to it, or maybe it to me. We drank each other in through every pore.

Taffy whined from the doorway. You have your own fur, Taffy; do not be jealous of mine.

I have the Sealskin wrapped around me like a cloak as I write in the Trophy Room. Poor Taffy doesn't know what to make of this new version of me. He thumps his tail but does not lie too near. Yes, Taffy, it may be that I am becoming a different creature and that soon you will not recognize me at all.

Soon, but not yet. I cannot turn myself into a Seal-maiden without warning Finian and Lady Alicia about Sir Edward. I cannot leave without saying good-bye. Soon I will restock my Folk Bag and walk the three miles along the cliffs to Firth Landing.

Everyone is away at the Harvest Fair, every servant, even the other dogs (for whom Sir Edward has doubtless bespoken the best rooms). It is unlikely that anyone will return before I do, but just in case, I will hide my Sealskin in the Cellar. It is too heavy to carry with me. No one would think to look there, and anyway, they're all too afraid.

I am very happy now, watching the rain fall in fat, hard strands. Have I ever been so happy?

The world is a magical place and I'm lucky to be alive in it. Did my mother watch the rain driving against these windows and think it beautiful?

Have I ever been so happy?

14

The *Harvest Fair*

August 18—the Harvest Fair

Something inside has sprung a leak. I am growing accustomed to the salt water dripping down my face. I lean over my paper to hide, but no one in the tavern looks my way. They stand around the fire and drink to the Harvest Fair and to the rain and to anything else they can think of.

No one pays attention to a serving girl.

I was transformed this morning, from savage to servant with a bar of soap and servants' clothes borrowed from Mrs. Bains's storeroom. A laced bodice and calico shift, very clean and almost new. I wonder if Corin's clothes would fit me now? I shall never be rosy and rounded—never like the Tragic Queen!—but if you squinted, you might almost take me for a young lady.

I left my hair for last, twisting it into a knot at my neck. And then—oh, I was clapped once more into an acorn shell. The singing spaces collapsed around me; gone were the echoes that paint the universe like shadows.

Imagine a world without shadows. You cannot touch a shadow, but a world without them is a hard world, and flat.

I didn't stumble once on the rough cliff-top walk to the Harvest Fair. Now that I know it's my hair that gives the world dimension and depth, I can manage without it. It's knowing the rules, I think.

It's as though you were standing in front of a mirror and tying a bow. If you know you're moving in a mirror world, if you know everything runs right to left, back to front, why then, you know how to adjust. You know to move your fingers opposite the way your mind tells them to go. But if you don't, you keep moving your fingers the wrong way and wonder why you can't even make the simplest knot.

The fairgrounds began at a grassy square in front of the Cathedral. The ground was a mass of mud, but the business of the first day was done, and the ale was flowing as freely as the rain, and certainly nobody seemed to mind.

Smoky flares shone off canvas booths pitched along the Cathedral walls. "Penny a pitch! Penny a pitch!" called the barker at the coconut shy. "All sharp!" A peddler with a whetstone, his cart hung with knives and axe blades.

The noise and cheer filled me with a delicious anticipation. I looked for Finian and I did not look for Finian.

The search itself was an event to savor. Here, smells of clove and nutmeg drifted from the spice stall. There, mounds of sugared almonds and candied cherries glistened beneath striped canvas. The stonecutter had set out a tray of cunningly carved animals. I lingered over a tiny quartz rooster, all swagger and strut.

"Perhaps your sweetheart will buy it for you!" called an unknown voice. A rush of laughter blew up from a knot of men. Blushing, and laughing too, I walked on. "A drink to the harvest!" Pewter tankards met with thuds of fellowship, warm ale sloshed over cold hands. "To the harvest!"

The crowd grew thin behind the Cathedral, the tents a little rumpled and shabby. "Who'll put his silver on this glossy fellow!" called a gloomy voice beneath a canvas, and a bright smell stained the air. It was a cockfight. I'd never find Finian there.

I was looking for Finian, only for Finian, confident my disguise made me invisible to anyone else. But when I turned away, I found a great beast with red ears blocking my way, asking politely for attention.

"Liquorice! Let me pass!"

"Liquorice!" Sir Edward called from the tent, not twenty feet behind.

"Go!" I pushed at Liquorice, felt the bony lumps of skull. "Your master's calling." If only my hair were loose, I could call upon the power of The Last Word and send him howling away.

"Who's your friend, Liquorice?" Sir Edward's voice brought back memories of fresh earth and mildew.

I stamped on Liquorice's foot; he yelped and slunk aside.

I imagined elegant Sir Edward at the fringe of that shabby company, staring as I disappeared round the other side of the Cathedral. Small growling shivers ran up my spine. I was splashed with mud to my knees and wet all over, straining myself back into the crowd. The stalls no longer tempted me, not the scented candles, the supple leathers, the crimson stitching in a lady's glove.

Sir Edward could not recognize me, I told myself. Not in a dress, not from the back. My Folk Bag—could he recognize my Folk Bag? But there are many leather bags in the world, and only one Corinna, whom he presumed to be dead.

The crowd flowed round a pretty bright-faced girl and her sweetheart, stopped in the middle of the lane. The man swung her close and kissed her full on the mouth. A most peculiar feeling overcame me; I was light-headed as though I might have a fever. When the couple moved on again, I saw it was the Valet, and in a red leather vest!

Now the crowd flowed around me, the crowd, together with flowing seconds and flowing thoughts and flowing hands, hands tightening round my waist, squeezing me through an alley between two stalls. Very delicately then, as though I were a waxen doll, the hands propped me against the Cathedral wall.

It was dark in there, but when I looked up, I still saw the familiar blue vein at the corner of Finian's eye. His voice was a shredded whisper. "You didn't run away to the Mainland!"

I felt none of the amazement I heard in my own voice.

"How did you recognize me?" I felt nothing much at all. The perfect doll, dress-up clothes over a waxen heart.

Finian reached for his handkerchief and peeled off his spectacles, which were foggy and beaded with rain. "I always recognized you." He swallowed hard, as though he'd bitten off too many words.

The wax doll was startled into life. A secret heart jumped at the dip of my throat; and all the lacings of my bodice couldn't stop a wild warmth rising from beneath.

"Have the Folk made mischief while I've been gone?" Oh, that I could simply melt away, like wax. Whatever I'd meant to say, it wasn't that.

"Rather a lot," said Finian. "Four cows died, and the hay wouldn't cure, just moldered away. But the oats and barley are safe, and that's something. The Folk have been quiet since the first week in August."

He shoved the spectacles back on his nose. "Your hair! How could it have grown so?"

"You forgot to wipe off the glass," I said.

"I can still see your hair. Oh, Corinna, where did you go?"

"Where did *you* go, that day on the pier?" I hadn't meant to say that, either, but the words had been swelling inside a long time, and now came bursting out.

Finian knew at once what I was speaking of. "I'm ashamed to say what I thought. But when I saw the *Windcuffer*, saw that she'd been tampered with . . ."

"Tampered?" I remembered sailing the *Windcuffer* in the storm, the inexplicable burst of water through the floorboards, fitting my fingers between them. "You thought I did it!"

"For revenge," said Finian. "Although I didn't know what I'd done to make you so angry."

"I would never harm the *Windcuffer*."

"Never?" said Finian, and I felt myself go red. "But when you set off after me, in the *Windcuffer*, I knew of course it wasn't you."

"Sir Edward!" The probability of this burst on me in a cold wave. He'd been worried about what Finian knew, worried he might not make a complacent stepson. "Trying to do away with you, just as he tried Midsummer Eve, pushing you from the cliffs."

I could say no more. My throat swelled with the notion that Finian thought I'd avenge myself on him; worse still, it could have been true. A silent rainfall of weeping overcame me.

Finian pressed a square of cambric into my hand. "I've gone back to saying my prayers every night like a good boy, praying for the chance to explain. To apologize."

I waited until I could speak. "I never use a handkerchief."

"Perhaps you never needed one until now."

"No, not much like Corin to need a handkerchief."

"You were never much like Corin," said Finian. "Lucky me, not to have been wearing my spectacles that first day we met. I missed the fine points of your appearance, but I wasn't fooled by them, either. I saw from the way you carried yourself that you were no boy."

"Even Sir Edward never guessed," I said. "People never think a Folk Keeper could be a girl."

"Not even Edward, and he's so clever, too!" Finian

said this so seriously, I was sure he must be laughing.

"Why did you never tell?" I said. "All these months, and you knew there was no Corin."

"Boredom, I suppose. If I told, all the excitement would be over at once. But I never thought it would be this exciting."

"It's more exciting than you know," I said. "It's my turn now to tell you Secrets. Did you know the Lady Rona was a Sealmaiden? That I'm her daughter?"

There was no room for a large person to be surprised; to start, or step back. Finian only whispered, as I had that night in the graveyard, "But the baby died at birth!"

"Lord Merton didn't want one of the Sealfolk as his heir and gave out that I'd died."

"I hear what you say," said Finian. "I even believe it. But I can't digest it." He pressed his fist to his middle as though he might have a bellyache. "How do you know this?"

"Sir Edward told me. He didn't want me as heir, either, so he dropped me through the Graveyard Shaft."

"The Graveyard Shaft! Yes, let's return to Edward. Tell me enough to hang him."

"He means to marry your mother."

"Ha!" said Finian. "He might have, six weeks ago. But now she disagrees with him on almost everything. It started when you vanished, which thoroughly upset our ways of thinking. I am to have a whole shipyard if I like!"

I have read and reread my account of that night in the churchyard. It was easy to remember and recount what Sir Edward had said during those long minutes I lay pressed into my own grave.

"Hanging's too easy," said Finian. "An axe might do better."

"Only if it's blunt," I said, thinking of my breathless fall through the Shaft.

"You're right," said Finian. "The old-fashioned ways have their charms. What do you say to drawing and quartering?"

I was a long time describing my days in the Twilight Cavern, my discovery of Old Francis, my starless night with the Folk.

"Do you mean to say you don't have the power of The Last Word!"

"I do now," I said, thinking back to early August. Hadn't Finian said that's when the Folk grew quiet?

"I don't know whether to be worried or relieved."

"Be both at once."

"Just tell me there's a happy ending," said Finian. "This Otherfolk story of yours is terrifying."

"It still hasn't ended, not until I return to the sea."

I still remember his look of—of what? Puzzlement? Astonishment? Anger? What right had he to be angry?

Just a thin slice of canvas away, a merchant was charging a young man too much for two blue ribbons. "They *will* go with brown hair?" the young man said. "You're *sure* they go with brown hair?"

"I see," said Finian. "You came to warn me. I'd rather hoped—oh, there's an end on it." He seemed to change the subject. "I began leaving the Cellar door ajar for Taffy. He must have known where you were all along, poor fellow. Couldn't you leave your own door ajar, Corinna? Go to the sea, just come back, too."

But I couldn't risk ending up like my mother, my Seal-skin stolen or destroyed. "What would I come back for?"

"For the Folk. For me. You could marry me."

He said this rather indifferently, but he peeled off his spectacles, and when he leaned forward, only our lips touched. Warm, hard fingers around my wrist; warm, soft lips against mine.

The press of air peeled away, and there came a moment of suspension, of liquid floating. I sank into those lips. I was still solid Corinna—I could feel it in the curious little shock that shivered through my middle—but like ice in water, I floated in my own liquid self.

And then my arm was flying wildly, connecting with his hand, with warm flesh and cold spectacles. The spectacles flew against the wall with a sharp crack, and I flew the other way, into the mud and clamor of the Harvest Fair. Finian could have caught me easily, but there came only his voice floating after.

"Listen to this. Corinna, listen! Midsummer Eve, the strands in my peat were silver!"

How I ran then! But I couldn't run as far as I wanted. A fisherman stationed at the foot of the cliff path advised me to take a wagon inland, as the rains had washed out a section of cliff. And so I did, with a crowd of Harvest revelers, two crying babies, and five chickens.

I wait now at this tavern for a farmer who's offered to take me the rest of the way in his cart—after he finishes his ale. I'd rather walk, but it would take me hours to reach the Manor, and my Sealskin.

All I can hear in my head is Finian's voice. *The strands in my peat were silver! Silver! Silver!*

August 18—later

Why didn't I go? Why didn't I seize my Sealskin this morning and plunge into the sea? Oh, foolish waiting, foolish human waiting. I wanted to warn Finian, I wanted to explain. I wanted to say good-bye. What a stupid thing to do—a stupid *human* thing! I swore I'd never let myself get caught as my mother had. And where has it left me? Trapped in the Caverns.

Should I have suspected something? But I'm sure everything was just as I'd left it, the doors to the Kitchens and Cellar ajar. At the top of the stairs, I pulled the pins from my hair. I needed no light to find my way to my Sealskin.

When I stepped into the inner Cellar, I felt at once a new texture, the fabric of the air pulled taut, as though . . . as though there'd been a candle recently burning. I swung my hair, reading the walls—*Poor Rona! Poor Rona!*—to the spot beside the Folk Door where I'd left my Sealskin.

In that instant, a flint scraped, a spark flared, a lantern cast a halo round Sir Edward and his angel smile.

I leapt for the Folk Door, hurled myself through. It slammed behind.

"Come out, Corinna." Sir Edward spoke through the Door. "It will be worse if I have to come after you."

"Come in, if you dare."

"Oh, I dare," said Sir Edward. "Didn't I snuff my candle when I heard you coming down the Cellar stairs? That should tell you I'm not afraid of the Folk."

That had been astonishingly brave. "Come in, then."

Sir Edward's footsteps drew near the Folk Door, paused. He did not dare.

I dived into my Folk Bag and lit a candle to start

writing. Have I not told myself things through my writing I hadn't thought of before? Hadn't I told myself I could find my way through the Caverns without a candle? What can I tell myself now?

Sir Edward cannot keep me trapped here; in two days, the others will return. Don't worry, Corinna. You can wait this out.

Why, then, am I terrified? Why have my bones turned to water? Am I melting, Corinna turned to liquid, trickling beneath the Door?

And why is Sir Edward laughing?

15

The *Harvest Fair* (Will It Never End!) Through the *Storms of the Equinox*

August 18—night of the Harvest Fair

I must have known somewhere deep inside why I could not wait it out. Why, too, Sir Edward might laugh.

"I have your Sealskin," he said. "The only question is how to destroy it. Fire, perhaps?"

I blew out my candle, as though to keep fire as far from me as possible. And there, in the dark, the spark of an idea flared.

"You think yourself powerful, don't you?" I cried, as scornfully as I could. "Listen to this: The night of the Storms, it was I who threw the skin of your jungle beast to the hounds."

"You!" Sir Edward said no more. He gave a piercing whistle, and soon I heard a soft panting outside the Folk Door.

"Liquorice is here with me," he said. "With me and your Sealskin. At it, lad!"

I sprang through the Folk Door, already casting a net of hair to gather The Last Word.

> *The story of a maiden fair,*
> *Sing briney, briney brink.*
> *With shades of silver in her hair,*
> *Sing briney, briney brink.*
> *Shut off forever from the sea,*
> *Consigned to Merton's company.*
> *Sing briney, briney brink,*
> *Sing briney, briney bonnie doon.*

Liquorice was screaming, a horrible dog scream, but I wouldn't stop. He'd already sprung at my Sealskin; let him feel the lash of my words.

> *She found her way to Cellar small,*
> *Sing briney, briney brink.*
> *And stabbed her name in floor and wall,*
> *Sing briney, briney brink.*
> *And now in snow and rain and cold,*
> *She lies alone beneath the mold.*
> *Sing briney, briney brink,*
> *Sing briney, briney bonnie doon.*

Sir Edward swung the lantern as though he would pitch it at me. "Liquorice!" I cried. "At him!" Poor Liquorice, under my spell, he could not disobey. "At him, lad!"

The lantern hurtled through the air. I sprang aside, but it was not intended for me. The fiery arc ended where Liquorice had been standing, spattering oil and light on my Sealskin.

I could not leap at once to its rescue. I gathered up my hair and held it in one hand. If my hair caught, I would flare like tinder and flicker out.

Fire sizzled over my Sealskin. I wore stout boots, stomped on the flames, but they'd spread already, they were everywhere. I fell to my knees, fire licked at my skirts, I beat at it with one hand. No good, that was no good. I leapt to my feet.

I let go my hair to free both hands and flipped the Seal-skin over. Fire flared bright in the gust of its movement, fire on my Sealskin, and on me, too. My skirts were still ablaze. I flung myself upon it, pressing the flames to the damp Cellar floor, suffocating also the flames lapping my skirts.

We were again in darkness.

When had Sir Edward begun screaming? "Fall off, lad!" I cried. Then silence, save for Liquorice panting, and little sobbing breaths from Sir Edward.

"Liquorice has broken my arm," he said presently.

"And to think," I said, "you didn't believe I had the power of The Last Word."

"What do you mean to do with me?"

"The Folk missed their sacrifice on the Feast of the Keeper," I said.

More silence. The door to the vegetable gardens slammed open, footsteps ran overhead.

"It's Finian," I said, sure that Sir Edward's ears were not as keen as mine. "Twice you tried and couldn't kill him."

"Midsummer Eve was mostly an accident," said Sir Edward, as though that excused everything. "I never tried after you disappeared. Old Francis, then you."

"Lady Alicia might have asked some hard questions," I said.

The footsteps were joined by a lantern, bobbing into the inner Cellar. I saw Finian in a new way with my hair loose, felt the motion of his neat and heavy bones, the particular way he displaced the air around him. The pattern of Finian, now woven inextricably into my hair.

He knelt beside me, reached out, for my hand perhaps, but drew back at the hurt to my palm. I didn't feel the pain yet. Strange, not to feel the pain. Finian did not speak. I could not see his eyes for the cracks in his spectacles and the lantern light shining off the glass.

More lanterns now, and anxious voices approaching, each overlapping the other in ragged counterpoint.

It was the Valet who hauled Sir Edward to his feet by the cravat he'd doubtless starched and pressed this morning. Lady Alicia held her lantern high, and I saw Sir Edward's face again in a halo of light. But instead of his angel smile, Sir Edward had begun to come apart like a tapestry man with a pulled thread, unraveling stitch by stitch, disintegration shivering through his face.

"He says his arm pains him," said Lady Alicia, disgusted.

"Oh, Mother," said Finian. "Corinna's the one who's hurt." I heard from his voice that he was weeping.

"My Sealskin," I said. "My Sealskin's hurt most of all."

Finian looked down, realizing now what it was I lay upon.

"I must see the damage to it," I said. Without a word, Finian lifted me from the Sealskin; the Valet held it before me.

I cannot erase the sight from my mind. In no place was it burned quite through, but it was a limp, pitiful thing, badly scorched in at least a dozen places.

"It's not destroyed," I said. "It may yet take me to sea."

But I can't try it for a long while; my burns are very bad. My left hand, and both legs. I wait now in the Music Room for the apothecary. It is futile to keep writing. There's no more to puzzle out; everything is clear in this new and bitter twist.

September 3

They thought I would die.

I know this, for black satin drapes the mirror to prevent Soulsucker passing through.

Don't waste your time, Soulsucker. Don't hang about, hungry for my soul. It is my own. I claim it, tattered and sorrowful as it is. Go away!

Two weeks and more have slipped away while I stayed inside my head, healing not just from my burns but also, I think, from the six-week darkness of the Caverns. Perhaps even from the four-year darkness of the Cellar. I remember a tin whistle playing quick, sad tunes, and Finian coaxing me to come out; and when I did creep out this morning, I thought it was still his voice I heard, coaxing, except why would he call me *My Lady*? And hadn't he also said he was going away?

I opened my eyes. It was Mrs. Bains who stroked my hand, entreated me to come out. I burst into tears.

"There, don't cry, My Lady. You've been ill a long time."

"Finian said he was leaving!" I sobbed. "I remember how he whispered it in my ear, told me I should wait."

"You heard that in your illness?" Mrs. Bains's little currant eyes blinked in surprise. "Don't you fret, My Lady. He and Lady Alicia will return soon."

It can't be very soon, however, as they have gone to Rhysbridge, to testify before the Great Courts that an heir with greater claim than theirs to Marblehaugh Park is still living. "They'll make it all proper and legal," said Mrs. Bains. "As for that horrid Sir Edward, he's fast in a Rhysbridge prison."

She couldn't understand why I would break out crying again. "Don't you worry about him, My Lady. He won't ever be back."

The world seemed unbearably sad. I suppose your heart can never really break, but I felt as though mine must have. I banged at my heart, which alarmed Mrs. Bains, less on account of my heart than my hand, which was wrapped in gauze and began to hurt. This new pain was comforting, taking the edge off the other.

Finian had to leave for me to realize I loved him. I loved him and he had gone away and soon I would try to leave, too, to join the Sealfolk. Even for Finian, I could not confine myself to land. My heart was with him, my heart was with the sea, and I knew which I would choose.

"I wish I were dead!" I said, which was foolish, as I

had no intention of dying. But people say foolish things all the time. Why shouldn't I?

"You're not to die!" said Mrs. Bains sharply, and snatched the black satin from the mirror. "We won't be needing this now."

My reflection surprised me. There were no more secrets. I was all Corinna, in a nightdress of ivory silk and a padded satin bed jacket, hair falling like water all about. With such a monstrous sleep, my hair should have grown to fill the room, but it has wearied of growing and stopped at a mere four feet.

"Very well," I said meekly. "I won't die."

Mrs. Bains sat beside me and ran her fingers through my hair. "Just like your mother's," she said. "I used to brush it for her, poor dear."

"I agree not to die," I said. "But I'll never agree to wear my hair up, like a lady."

But I had misread her thought. "Never!" she said. "I know what it was to your mother, loose like that. Oh, don't think I don't know what your hair is to you, being of the Sealfolk. How without it you lose your balance. How after your twelfth birthday it becomes another set of eyes."

"After your twelfth birthday?" I said.

"Isn't that the way of it, that you grow into the power of your hair?"

But I wouldn't know. I cut my hair before I turned twelve. No wonder its powers came as a surprise.

"And it gives you the power of The Last Word," I said.

"Your mother said nothing about that."

But she must have had that power, staying as she did in

the Cellar. Otherwise, how could she have escaped harm?

The Last Word: It is yet another gift from my mother.

September 5

I awoke this morning with a broken heart, which broke again after Mrs. Bains showed me my Sealskin.

I'd had a sudden piercing hope: If I could heal, perhaps my Sealskin could, too. After all, it had grown as I had grown.

But after I bullied Mrs. Bains to hold the Sealskin up before me, I had to turn my face away.

"We want you here with us, My Lady," said Mrs. Bains, as though that might console me. "This is where you belong." Then, seized with inspiration, "The autumn Storms will be upon us soon. What will we do then, with no Folk Keeper?"

But she had to admit that for now the Folk are quiet. Still smarting, perhaps, from the lash of The Last Word.

"Where is Taffy?" I said suddenly.

Mrs. Bains had to think. She didn't know.

No one knew. No one has seen him for a long time.

It will be better for the pain if I walk the corridors.

September 6

Taffy was in the first place I looked.

I insisted on going alone, although they all said the Valet should help me on the Cellar stairs. I have a surprising companion, however: Liquorice. Poor hounds, I pity them, adrift in a world without Sir Edward.

No Folk Keeper ever looked as I did, green velvet skirts dusting the stone, lace very white by candlelight. Mrs. Bains has tried to make me into a proper lady, and for now I have submitted, given in to petticoats and shifts, to velvets and brocades. I was Corin for long enough. I shall see who else I might be.

I paused at the entrance to the inner Cellar. Damp seeped through my embroidered slippers. The smell came to me first, all but forgotten from the Caverns. Damp bone, with a whiff of decay. I closed my eyes.

I closed my eyes, but I couldn't escape the picture that tangled with my hair. I couldn't escape the image of the skeleton—if you could call it so. The bones were mostly splinters now, crushed by wild, wet mouths. Taffy had been old and brittle. Old Francis, at least, had kept his form, his mournful, bony smile. But there was not enough left of Taffy for that. Perhaps just a slice in the air where his smile had once been.

Folk, consider yourselves warned: I'll stand for no damage during these Storms. You've already had your sacrifice, and if you grow wild, you will hear from me!

I buried him in the churchyard. The headstone marking baby Corinna's grave had been removed; it was easy to dig the loose mold. I eased Taffy into the earth, and although it was impossible to rearrange him, I still take comfort in my last picture of his bones, in the way he burst the darkness in a brilliant constellation of himself.

Something better than stone marks his grave. He lies under dozens of amber beads, all glowing in the cool autumn sun.

September 19

I was looking the wrong way when they arrived at last.

I sat on the cliffs with Liquorice tonight, clutching at the heather, for the wind was growing stronger, blowing in all directions, and always in my face. Liquorice and I realized in the same moment they were coming up behind us. But I grew stony still, while he leapt to his feet and stood wagging the tip of his tail.

"She pretends she doesn't notice us!" said Finian.

I had to turn around then, and wag my own tail, and maybe even smile, which I did not feel like at all.

"Don't get up," said Lady Alicia, sinking down beside me. "You have the best seat in all of Marblehaugh Park." She leaned over and kissed my cheek.

"It's all very well for two ladies to embrace," said Finian. "But what's a poor gentlemen to do?"

"You could shake her hand," said Lady Alicia.

"I'd rather take it." This he did, very gently, studying my palm, the blistered redness now puckering to scars. "And you've transformed again! Don't make me work so hard to recognize you."

"I hardly recognize myself." I thought of the stranger in my mirror tonight, brocade skirts shot with pewter threads, stiff silver pleats at the bodice, which suddenly seemed cut too low. "You have new spectacles."

"Yes, someone broke mine."

"You look like the mistress of Marblehaugh Park." Lady Alicia was both more beautiful than I remembered, and more worn. I could almost believe now she was the mother of a grown son.

"You shall be mistress here, not me," I said.

"Help me, Mother," said Finian. "Tell her she can't go."

"I will do no such thing," said Lady Alicia.

"Then tell her we have a proposal. We do have a proposal for her, don't we, Mother?"

"That's one way of putting it." Lady Alicia set a black velvet box on my lap. "But Finian must do the proposing."

"Open it!" said Finian. "Maybe it will propose by itself."

It opened with a little snap. Inside lay a band of opals and emeralds, the colors of the sea. I tipped it into the smooth palm of my right hand.

Waves slapped at the cliffs below, somewhere a curlew cried.

"This is where I leave." Lady Alicia rose. "Finian, you shall have to fend for yourself."

"Deserted by my own mother!" Finian laid his hand over mine, trapping the ring between our two palms. "This will come out all wrong, as I can never manage to be quite serious, but here it is: I want to marry you!"

He shook his head and laughed. "No, this is where I should start: I love you. I love you with your stubbornness and conviction and eye for small beauties; and now that you have the power of The Last Word . . . Well, I'm glad I'm not one of the hounds!"

How could I answer that! Finian sighed. "Not very romantic, I suppose."

"I like your sort of romance," I said slowly. "I couldn't do with the on-your-knees-in-the-moonlight kind. But it's difficult to speak of love. I haven't the habit; I've gone my whole life without."

"Three words," he said. "Try it. The pain will only last a moment."

That Finian! He could always make me smile. This time, I even let it show on my face.

"I love you."

Finian took a deep breath. "So you will stay!"

How could I explain? "Remember how it was when you were forbidden to be building ships or thinking of a life with the sea? I have a life with the sea, too, but you'd have me confined to land by a promise of love, or marriage?"

"Why does it have to be one over the other?" said Finian. "Live in the sea if you like, only come back again. I'd wait for you, every evening."

I shook my head. "A Sealmaiden lives in the sea; that is her proper life."

"You don't know that, Corinna. Once you were convinced that being a Folk Keeper was your proper life. You're so one-sided, not even considering the idea."

"You said you like me stubborn."

"So I did." Then, very irritated, "You won't miss me?"

"I will. But if I stayed, I'd miss myself more."

Finian's hand still lay across mine. I drew mine away. Our hands were pressed so tight together, the ring left twin half-moon smiles on my palm.

He closed his fingers around it. "When do you leave?"

"After the Storms. I'll see the Folk make no mischief."

"At least a week, then," said Finian.

"The Storms are coming early, tomorrow perhaps."

Finian shook his head, but I know what I know, for my eyes are fierce and bright and my hair can see the shadow of the wind.

I've sprung another leak. My paper is wet and the lead is smudging. But a few more drops of salt won't make a bit of difference to the sea. The cry of a tin whistle drifts through the night. Play all the sad songs you like, Finian. I'll never change my mind.

September 24

These may be the last words I ever write. I am on the cliffs, halfway to the sea. Liquorice senses something is not as usual. He lies sphinx-like, four legs tucked beneath, ready to spring. I'm sorry, Liquorice. You can't come where I'm going.

I will leave my Journal beneath a heavy stone by the cliff path. It's been months since it was a proper Folk Record. There will be a new Folk Keeper at the Manor, and he shall have to keep his own Record and learn his own ways of tending the Folk.

I have said my good-byes, almost wordless, all of them. Lady Alicia's face was crumpled, as though she'd not rested well. The late light shone off Finian's spectacles, turning him into a cipher.

I embraced Lady Alicia. We are new at this, and it is awkward. But how much more awkward to shake hands with Finian, my hand in his, his swallowing mine. I leave behind this ridiculous custom of hands pumping up and down. All meaningless. Up and down, up and down.

I've written almost to the end of this Folk Record, begun so long ago, at Candlemas. I have reached the end of my human words and have nothing more to say.

16

A New First Page

September 25

The Sealfolk are calling me; I will join them soon. This is the first page of my new book, my new life. I love the heady feeling of putting words on paper, ink now, my own wet, black letters. A world of ink, and air to dry it, too. I shall never finish my story.

I can only try to keep up with myself, starting with last evening, when I stood on the beach, my Sealskin bundled in my arms. The wind was strong, trailing behind it a pale ribbon of geese. The sea skittered into whitecaps, my hair whipped round me as I dropped my cloak to the ground.

I peeled off Lady Corinna Merton in layers. Now overskirt and petticoat. Now under-petticoat and bodice.

It never ends, this business of being a lady. I raised my shift over my head, feeling the salt air touch me, feeling newly alive, as though I'd been swaddled in cotton wool all my life and was just now beginning to breathe.

I stood there a long moment, wrapped in the salty twilight, then draped the Sealskin round my shoulders. It looked weary, ravaged, but still it fell exactly from shoulder to heel. I held it closed at the neck.

I was ready, toes pale as shells curling over the edge of the beach, the waves at high tide slapping me with wet. The sea frothed out before me; bits of sky shone through a tattered moon.

I closed my ears, shut myself into my own head. I could hear myself swallow then, hear the thud of my heels when I stepped back, then bounced forward to jump. I collapsed my lungs, leaving all air behind.

The seal-change did not overtake me at once. The weight of the Sealskin eased from my shoulders, but that was only the ordinary magic of the buoyant sea. When I looked back at myself, I was still all Corinna. I still had arms and legs, which I still had to kick to move through the water. I still had to hold the Sealskin at the neck; it drifted behind me like a cape.

The direction of the Seal Rock was built into my bones, unalterable, as perfect pitch might be built into another. I skimmed the pearl-light water, a mixture of moon and sea. My hand was a pale starfish, clearing a path for myself, the sea-light turning blue veins to green. Shooting-star fish arched before me.

I followed the descending slope of the seafloor, gliding over the scatter of rocks I'd often seen at low tide. But everything came alive underwater. The rockweed and wrack swelled into swaying gardens in the watery wind. The crabs had crept from hiding, and the delicate feet of sea urchins waved slowly about.

Deeper I sank, where the moonlight couldn't follow. But the sea shrugged herself against me, and that brought light enough. There was a new pressure of water against cheek. Was the water heavier? Thicker? No, I was going faster than before.

Two starfish hands stretched before me: The Sealskin clung to my body of itself. Moments ago I'd been groping about, digging a tunnel through the water. But now my hands needed only to steer. In a flashing series of images, echoes of an unfamiliar shape met my streaming hair behind.

What did I see in this watery canvas? I saw the new alignment of my feet, no longer neat *L*s at my ankles but curving extensions of what had once been legs. I saw the fan-shaped spread of them, the fans moving rhythmically together and apart, shooting me in my own bright trajectory through the sea.

I painted a new path that angled sharply upward, broke through a skim of moonlight into air. The change had begun at my feet. There was the sweep of Corinna's bluish skin from shoulder to thigh. But webbed flippers fused what could no longer be called ankles and smooth fur bound my legs above the knee.

What had been double was becoming single. The Sealskin still had the power to transform; not even fire could strip that away.

My slow underwater heart sprang into land speed as I

watched with fascination, and a kind of horror. My Seal-skin was taking me over. Silvered fur stretched, swallowing skin, binding thigh to thigh.

I glanced back to shore. A lantern shone from the cliff. Was Finian watching for me there? The Sealskin yawned over hip bones, sharp as knives. *Once you thought being a Folk Keeper was your proper life*, Finian had said. Was this what I wanted after all?

I pulled at the Sealskin. Such a relief: It peeled back easily. Should I let it take me over? As Finian had said, it needn't be one over the other. I could always come back.

I hung in the wind-torn waves. The Sealskin crept up my side, wrapped round my middle. And then, when I was more seal than human . . .

My words vanished. I could no longer shape an image of inky wetness, spitting up pearls. I could no longer name Finian, couldn't even pretend I didn't love him.

An aching desolation overcame me. Gone was my new power of sculpting images with rhythm, welding rhythm to rhyme. Gone, too, was my newest power: saying those three words Finian had coaxed from me.

My hands moved of themselves, pulled at the Seal-skin. I couldn't go on before I knew I could retrieve my words. The seal-shape melted away, powerful muscles yielding to a pale belly. As my words came flooding back, so did a searing pain, fire in water.

The Sealskin clung fast to my thigh. I touched the spot; it had been burned there. I had the words now, I could tell my story even as it unfolded. The Sealskin could reverse the fusion of seal to human flesh, but not where it had been burned. The fire had seared all that away.

I wanted myself back. I tore at the Sealskin, ripping it from me, which ripped away Corinna, too. Raw flesh, oozing blood, my own faraway scream.

Five more burned patches showed on the seal part of me below. Perhaps the Sealfolk shrugged their Sealskins from them as a dog shakes water. But to get mine off, I needed to rip at it, which would be impossible once the seal-change took over my hands. If I became a Seal-maiden, I'd stay a Sealmaiden. The Sealskin was no longer a two-way door between land and water.

Quick! The Sealskin peeled away to the next burned patch. I closed my ears against my screams. Now, three more patches, now two. Thank the Saints I had my words. I could name the bitter taste rising from my stomach, describe the arc of pain.

A final savage tearing, a final sickening surrender. My Sealskin floated free. On the water, now in the water, the sea pulling it into herself.

The waves slapped at me. I was so weary. It was hard not to surrender, to follow my Sealskin into the unlighted regions.

The waves smashed at me, and only now I noticed: I had brewed my own little tempest. *Three drops of Sealfolk blood.* A storm, with the Manor so far away, and me in such a fire of pain!

I clung to the waves, weeping. Then all at once, silvery heads rose all around. I had called the Sealfolk to me. Or perhaps they'd come of themselves, as they had the last time I'd raised a storm.

"I want to go home!" I opened my arms. The smallest

of them swam into my embrace, and together, we all sank beneath the churning world.

We left the storm behind. The sea whispered and murmured against me, the Sealfolk speeded me home. It was humbling and comforting to be one tiny piece of this intense life. *So one-sided*, Finian had said. He was right. I needn't become a Sealmaiden to have a life with the sea. I was a part of it already, and best of all, I could still have my own words.

My mother went mad when her Sealskin was destroyed. She turned her back forever on the sea. She may never have known her powers, that the sea was open to her still. But I won't go mad; I'll make the sea my second home. This is how we are different.

There was the coming-home thrill as the Sealfolk and I drifted up the rocky incline near shore, old landlocked territory seen newly underwater. There was the dark pressure of the beach just beyond, and a memory of surfacing here Midsummer dawn, bearing Finian like a bubble.

My head broke into the thin air. The storm had all but passed. There was Finian, scrambling down the cliff. He should mind his feet; there, he almost fell. On the beach lay a pile of velvet and lace belonging to Lady Corinna Merton.

I attached myself to the land with my fingertips; high tide rose to the very edge of the beach. The Sealfolk gathered in a half-moon around me. We gazed at each other; Finian set loose a landslide of pebbles.

I was not quite laughing, not quite crying. "I'm not one of you, but I'm not Lady Corinna, either. Let me come with you sometimes. I know how to call you."

I turned back to land when the Sealfolk turned back to sea, curling both hands over the edge of the beach, my head rising just above. Both in and out of the water, I waited. Finian was running now, my cloak bundled in his arms, and I had already chosen my Conviction.

Acknowledgements

Many thanks to all my readers, whose generous criticism helped me make this the best book I possibly could.

To the members of my wonderful writing group, who read an excruciating number of drafts: Esther Hershenhorn, Phyllis Mandler, Harriette Gillem Robinet, Myra Sanderman, and Linda Schwab.

Also to Julie Billingsley, Pat Billingsley, Ruth Billingsley, Toni Buzzeo, Julia Halpern, Suzanne Lewis, Dian Curtis Regan, and Natalie S. Wainwright. Belated thanks to Natalie for the gift of the title *Well Wished*.